LA\

CONFESSIONS OF A
CONTRACT KILLER

ONE TEAM PUBLISHING & FILMS
Published by One Team Publishing & Films
Nashville, Tennessee 37216, USA
www.oneteam615.com

Copyright © Layla Lowe, Edgar Alan Cole, 2016

ALL RIGHTS RESERVED

ACKNOWLEDGEMENTS:
I would like to take this opportunity to thank my family, my children and of course Ed
Cole and One Team, for believing in me and making it possible for me to follow my
dreams. The support and encouragement I have had from my family and children have
been exceptional. I have been on a journey writing this book. It has brought out the best
in me as well as the worst at times. I want to thank my friends and work colleagues for
putting up with me, while I spoke about this book repeatedly. Ed Cole showed me the
way, and I followed. He advised me and put me in my place, when I went off track. Ed
reassured me when I thought my work wasn't good enough, and for that I will always be
grateful. I am very lucky to have the most beautiful, intelligent and loving children
whose encouragement led me to finish this book. I feel blessed to have you all in my life
and thank you all for everything.

REGISTERED TRADEMARK-Edgar Alan Cole, 2014

Printed in the United States of America

Without limiting the rights under copyright reserved above, no part of this publication
may be reproduced, stored in or introduced into a retrieval system, or transmitted, in
any form, or by any means (electronic, mechanical, photocopying, recording, or
otherwise), without the prior written permission of both the copyright owner and the
above publisher of the book.

PUBLISHER'S NOTE

This is a work of fiction. The names, characters, places, and incidents either are the
product of the author's imagination or are used fictitiously, and any resemblance to
actual persons, living or dead, business establishments, events, or locales is entirely
coincidental. The publisher does not have any control over and does not assume any
responsibility for author or third-party Web sites or their control. If you purchased this
book without a cover you should be aware that this book is stolen property. It was
reported as "unsold and destroyed" to the publisher and neither the author or publisher
has received any payment for this "stripped book." The scanning, uploading, and
distribution of this book via the Internet or via any other means without the permission
of the publisher is illegal and punishable by law. Please purchase only authorized
electronic editions, and do not participate in or encourage piracy of copyrighted
materials. Your support of the author's rights is appreciated.

DEDICATION

To

My mother who I hope is looking down on
me from heaven and my two beautiful
children.

Margaret,
Thankyou for your Support
Happy reading!
lots of love
Leanne
AKA Cayla lenne

CONTENTS

INTRODUCTION

Everyone in this world has a beginning that shapes the person he or she will be, even contract killers. Jack grew up in a council flat in Brixton London, with his big sister Amy, his druggie mother Irene, and alcoholic father Jimmy. Life wasn't easy. If it wasn't for his big sister looking out for him, God only knows how he would have survived. His sister was more like a mother to him. She protected him as a young child, which in a way made him the man he became. From a very young age Jack was taught that it was a dog- eat-dog world that he lived in. He saw everything that any usual parents wouldn't want their child to see. His parents were complete wasters, and his dad was a violent alcoholic who thought that the world owed him a living.

Jack's mum was a stereotypical, abused house wife/victim. She took his dad's abuse and hid her feelings with prescription drugs. And when they became too weak for her, she moved on to the harder street drugs, which she would pay for in anyway necessary. Jack always thought that his parents were never meant to be parents at all. Neither of them had a maternal or paternal instinct.

He can't remember one birthday party, one school trip, or even a Monday morning, when he would go to school with dinner money in his pocket. Whatever he had he got it from his sister. She learnt to shop lift at a young age, and every piece of clothing he had was down to her quick fingers. She was arrested a few times but always got off with a caution. Everyone knew that she was only doing what she had to do, for her and her brother to survive. Amy taught him right from wrong and always made him pray with her, after she had a shoplifting spree. She taught him that some things had to be done for the good of others. For example, she stole to feed them and clothe them. Amy never stole for fun, and she always asked God for forgiveness and confessed her actions to him, either at confession or in a prayer.

As soon as she was old enough, Amy made sure she had a job and continued to look after her brother. However, Jack grew into a man to be reckoned with. He took it upon himself to protect his sister, from the nasty world they lived in and the nasty people they came across, including their dad. Jack hated his parents, but he was glad they were his parents as it was them that made him a fighter. It was them that taught him how to hate, how to despise, and how to manifest those feelings to make them work for you. He worked his way from security to second in charge in no time at all, thanks to the employment and eventual friendship of Benny.

Benny was a known face and taught Jack everything he knew. He was good at what he did, and he liked who he had become. The only problem was that Jack saw his brutal murders and torturous endings of other's lives as a good thing. According to him he only killed the bad. So in around about way, he was doing good. Jack always confessed his sins to his God who was the ultimate boss in his world.

However sometimes Jack felt that God was taking the piss, because he was clearing the world of evil. But God was bringing evil closer to home! That wasn't what Jack had signed up for; no-one hurt his family. That shit was personal and made Jack question his faith, which of course was a dangerous scenario. Jack with a faith and a purpose in life was scary. But Jack with no faith, no purpose, and no reasoning behind his actions was damn right madness!

PART I

THE KILLER

CHAPTER 1

BORN INTO EVIL

When Irene met Jimmy, she was totally swept off her feet. He was tall with dark hair, and he had this look about him that just sent shivers down her spine. Irene was a looker herself. Everyone noticed her. She was tall, blonde with a decent cleavage, and a great arse. She met his gaze one night in a pub. They didn't have to speak, and the sexual tension between them said it all. That was the best night of passion she had ever experienced. Jimmy made her feel beautiful. He kissed her from her toes to her lips, and he spread her legs and let his tongue explore her wet vagina. Irene had never experienced anything like it, and she couldn't control herself. Her body was flowing with juices that she didn't even know existed. She was moaning and grabbing his head telling him to give it to her. And when he did, Irene screamed with pleasure, held his pert arse in her hands, and pushed him harder towards her. She couldn't get enough of him, and then they climaxed together. She looked up at him and told him that she loved him. That was it; she was smitten.

When Irene found out she was pregnant with Amy, she was happy. She thought it would seal their love. Irene practically ran to the pub to find him, and she walked in all flushed and sweaty. She saw her Jimmy at the bar with some girl. The girl was a brunette with long hair and a tight dress on. Irene thought she couldn't of looked cheaper if she had tried. Irene called to Jimmy. He clearly didn't hear her, as he would never have ignored her. She walked over to him and said, "Babe, I need to talk to you." Jimmy looked at her like he had never seen her before, and his response shocked her. "Can't you see I am fucking busy?" She looked at him with her big blue eyes, beginning to fill up with tears. Irene again told him, "I need to talk to you." "And I need a drink with my new friend here. So do me a favour love, go home."

The brunette looked her up and down and laughed at her. She looked so fucking smug. Irene couldn't control herself. She jumped up and grabbed the bitch's hair with both her hands. She was shouting, "Who the fuck are you looking at, you little slut?" Irene went nuts. She pulled her head down towards her knee, as she brought it up to smack her in the face. Her nose exploded all over Irene's jeans. Suddenly Jimmy was picking her up and pulling her away. He asked her, "What's your problem you mad fucking bitch?" Jimmy took her outside and shook her hard. "What are you fucking playing at you dozy mare?"

Irene was crying more with anger than anything else. "I'm fucking pregnant Jimmy." Jimmy looked dumbstruck. "What did you say?" "I said I'm pregnant, and I am having your baby. I am having our baby." "Are you taking the piss? Is this a fucking joke?" "No babe, I'm not joking. We are having a baby. Ain't you pleased?" " Do I look fucking pleased?" He was devastated, realising that this meant he was now stuck with this chick. Jimmy liked fucking her. But apart from that, he thought she was as thick as shit. And he wanted to knock her out every time she spoke. Her high-pitched voice and childish conversations sent him crazy.

However he knew he now he had to marry the little slapper and quick smart. His mother wouldn't take too kindly to having a grandchild out of wedlock. He would never hear the end of it. Jimmy didn't agree much with the Catholic religion, especially the no sex out of wedlock shit. But he did agree that abortion was a no-no. He now had no fucking choice but to marry this silly tart and accept that she will be his future, her and some fucking kid. Jimmy couldn't believe his bad luck. He married her, because that was the right thing to do. Jimmy didn't want to marry her; he didn't even want to see her anymore. He was a young man who wanted to fuck everything with tits. But there he was, saddled with a dumb bimbo and a fucking baby. Jimmy was so pissed off, and he decided to show her who was boss, on their wedding night.

He told her straight that she had a duty to please him, and from now on she done as she was told. Irene thought he was joking. She even laughed at him. But when she looked at Jimmy, she realised he was being serious. And that was the moment she realised marrying him was the biggest mistake of her life. The beatings started a little while after the wedding. At first she blamed herself. Jimmy didn't mean to hurt her. It was her fault for not doing his dinner properly or leaving creases in his shirts. She told him she would get better at being his wife; that she would try harder; but it was no good. He had made up his mind how this marriage was going to work, and he was the boss. Jimmy dominated everything, from how she dressed to the colour of her hair. Irene slowly changed into a door mat.

She learnt not to have an opinion, she learnt to agree with everything he said and ultimately she learnt that she would never be good enough, not for him or anyone. She started taking Diazepam and anything else she could get her hands on from pain killers to sleeping pills. Anything that would make her feel numb. She lived for that feeling cause then she could block out the world especially her husband. Irene gave birth to Amy when she was 21 years old. She looked at her beautiful baby girl in her arms. Amy looked so innocent, so small, and so sweet. But Irene felt nothing. She didn't instantly love her like everyone said she would. In fact all Amy was to her was a reminder of her mistakes. She looked around the hospital ward and couldn't wait to leave. The walls were all white, and it was full of screaming babies, perfect fucking wives, and perfect fucking mums. She hated it. However Irene put her face on and pretended to be the happiest woman in the world. That way she would be able to leave quicker. The only bonus about being there was the easy access to pain killers and any other pill she could get her hands on, when the dozy fat nurse wasn't paying attention.

Things got worse when Irene took Amy home to her two-bed flat, which was situated in the middle of a Brixton council estate. She hoped having Amy would build bridges between her and her husband. Irene hoped the baby would bring them closer together. She couldn't of been more wrong. Jimmy would go out on the piss until all hours. And if that baby dared to wake him up, Irene would get a slap. If she was lucky, that is all she would get. But on a bad day she would be beaten until she actually felt like she was going to die. He would kick her, stamp on her, pull her hair, slap her, and even bite her. Jimmy would shout at her telling her that she was a nasty whore; she was ugly and fat; and she was a joke of a wife and a fucking shit mum.

Irene would beg him to stop, but this seemed to just make him angrier. So she would guard her face, turn on her side in the foetal position, and take her punishment. Irene told herself it was her punishment for being a shit wife, for putting on weight, and for not being able to please her husband. She hated herself more than he hated her. Irene would eventually pass out. When she came round, he would have Amy in his arms, feeding her or doing something equally as fatherly. He would talk to Irene in a sweet voice, tell her to go get in the bath, and clean herself up a bit. After all she didn't want to scare the baby now did she? Irene would do as she was told.

From when Amy could walk and talk, she practically brought herself up. Her dad was always out on the piss, and her mum was always off her face. When her dad was home, she knew to stay quiet. Most of the time Amy would already be asleep. But on the occasions that she wasn't, she knew not to move, not to make daddy angry, or mummy would get hurt again. Amy would hide under her bed when the drama started between her parents. No one checked on her or even wondered where she was. She learnt to love her own company, to entertain herself, play by herself, talk to herself, and dress herself. Anything she needed she would need to get it for herself.

Amy took to Jack as soon as he was born, and she felt like his mum in many ways. She would change his nappy and feed him his bottle. Their mum just used to hand him over, like you would hand someone the TV remote. Their mum didn't want to be pregnant with Jack. If the truth was known, Irene didn't even want to take part in conceiving him. In her mind that husband of hers had taken her life from her. More kids was just his way of keeping her, holding her back from ever following her dreams. Her life had turned in to nappies, screaming kids, dodging fists, and taking pills. Irene got most of her drugs from the actual doctor. She made up a back problem for which he would prescribe painkillers. Irene then told him she had trouble sleeping because of the pain, and he would prescribe sleeping tablets.

She would then say she lost the prescription, or that she was going on holiday to enable her to get another prescription or a bigger stash. It was only the odd occasion she would seek the stronger stuff. Irene would only occasionally treat herself to a bit of coke. That really took the edge off. It made her feel like she was on top of the world. Irene never had much cash, so she would often pay for it in kind. It didn't bother her. She was used by her husband often and brutally taken against her will. So what difference did it make to have quick shag with some stranger? In her head it made no difference at all, especially after she took that first line.

Jack looked up to his sister. He loved everything about her. She had long blonde hair, big blue eyes, and legs that went on forever. Amy really was beautiful. Jack was about 6-years-old when he really understood what was going on. Amy and Jack were playing hide and seek one day, when they heard their dad's key turn in the lock. It was too late for Amy to warn Jack, and Jack had no choice but to stay in his mum's wardrobe, where he had been hiding in the game. He heard the screams and crying coming from the front room. He knew it was his mum. Jack knew she was being hurt, but he also knew that was normal in this house. That's what dads did. Jimmy was screaming at her, "Wake up you fucking junkie slag! What the fuck do you think this is a fucking doss house? I said fucking wake up you little slut!" Irene pretended to be asleep as he slapped her in her face. Then it suddenly went quiet, and Jack was even more scared by the silence. He peeped through the wardrobe door and saw no one. He suddenly thought about Amy and wondered where she was. Did she know Dad was back? Was she still counting facing the bedroom wall, so he could run and hide?

He opened the wardrobe door wider and decided he needed to go and find Amy. He crept across the bedroom and reached the bedroom door which led to the hall way. The flat wasn't big and the narrow hall led to every room. Opposite his mums bedroom was the bedroom he shared with Amy. The door was slightly open and he could sense movement inside. He sighed with relief it must be Amy, she must still be looking for him. He ran across the hall way and through the bedroom door, he looked up to see his dad standing over Amy with his trousers down. Amy was lying on the floor naked. Why was she naked? Why were dad's trousers down? Why was Amy crying? What was going on?

His dad suddenly turned to look at Jack. He instantly pulled up his trousers and shouted at Jack, "Get out of here you little fucker." But Jack couldn't leave, because his Amy was upset. So he instinctively ran to her. He chucked himself on top of her to give her a big cuddle, which always made her feel better. She squeezed him tight and sobbed. Jack looked up at his dad and couldn't help but say, "What have you done to Amy?" He realised his dad hadn't moved. Jimmy just stood there in silence watching them. After 30 seconds or so, he just walked out of the bedroom.

Jack whispered to Amy, "It's OK. He has gone. You are ok now Ames." Amy kissed his forehead and said, "Thanks Jackie my little hero." Jack didn't know what she meant, but he guessed she was pleased with him. Amy got dressed slowly, as her body hurt all over. "Are you ok Amy?"

"Yes bro. I will be OK, because you saved me. You saved me from that monster dad of ours, and I am so lucky to have you." "Amy, I am lucky cause you are my big sister, and we look after each other remember. You said that no matter what we stick together. I will never leave you Ames; I won't let the monster get you again." Amy looked at her little brother with so much love that she could burst. He was a sweet boy; he was more grown up for his age. Jack was intelligent and cute, and she simply loved the bones of him.

She found herself thinking that as long as she had her Jack, that monster could do what he wanted to her. Amy would always protect her little brother. Jack broke her chain of thought. "Amy, what did he do to you?" Amy cuddled her brother, "Don't worry about it Jack. I'm OK now." "Amy, I am a big boy now, and I want you to tell me." She knew he would work it out in the end, but she just didn't want to say it. Amy began to sob, and Jack cuddled her and let her cry.

He rubbed her back and stroked her hair. "Amy please tell me." "All you need to know Jack is that our dad is a monster. He hurts me. He hits me and makes me touch him in places I don't want to. He hurts my girl parts." She took a breath and looked at Jack's facial expression. "It hurts Jack. It makes me hurt for days."

Amy then broke down, and Jack took her once more into his arms. "I hate it. He hurts me, and I hate him." Amy sobbed for what seemed like ages. Jack stayed silent. He was thinking about what his sister had said. Jack had seen things like that on the TV when everyone was asleep, and he sneaked into the front room to watch TV. The girls always screamed on the TV too. So Amy must be really hurt, which made him cry for his Amy. They cried together. "Jack, I promise you that when I get big, I will get a job, get some money, and we can run away. I won't ever leave you Jack, never."

"Ok Amy. I will come with you. But when I am big, I promise you that I will kill the monster." For some reason that made Amy laugh a real belly laugh. Jack joined in, and they laughed and laughed until they actually forgot what they were laughing about, and their ribs ached.

Jack sat in silence, as he watched his big brave sister brush her hair out. He loved his sister, and it was at that moment, aged just 6-years-old, that he decided he would always be her hero. He would always protect her, no matter what. From that day onwards when his dad came home drunk, Jack refused to hide. Instead he threw himself on his sister to protect her. Most of the time this meant that they both got beats, but Jack didn't care anymore. He took his beats like a soldier. Jack would never cry in front of his dad, even at his young age. He refused to let his dad see any weakness in him.

Jack grew up hating Jimmy. He hated him for what he did to his sister, and he hated him for the beatings he dished out. Jack hated him for not leaving and staying gone. His hate for his father grew like a cancer. The hate became his obsession. As Jack got older, he would daydream about killing him. He would create every scenario in his head about the best way to kill his dad, the best way to protect his sister from that wanker. Jack didn't give a shit about his mum.

Irene spent most of her life out of it on prescription drugs, sleeping on the sofa. She rarely got dressed, and she lived in her pyjamas. As far as he was concerned, Amy was the only one he loved and the only one that meant anything to him. She cooked for him; she would shoplift his school uniform and decent trainers for him; so he didn't feel out of place at school. Amy would help him with his homework and pander to his every need when he was sick. He owed his Ames everything. Jack would protect her as long as he lived, no matter what it took and no matter how hurt he got in the process.

When jack entered his teenage years, he got a lot bigger. He was tall and Hench. Jack reminded Amy of a warrior. Her little soldier had grown into a warrior. He was actually built like a brick shit house. There was nothing small about him at all. Jack was a fighter too. No one would cross Jack from the age of about 15. Everyone knew he was a brawler. Amy was so proud of him. He had grown into a handsome man, and he would look out for her all the time, whether it be at home or in the streets. Jack was her protector. This only became a bit awkward when she started to have boyfriends. She knew Jack would vet them behind her back. And if he didn't like them, they would end up with a fat lip and a black eye. They would tell Amy they didn't want to see her anymore.

Amy knew Jack had kicked them in and warned them off, but she couldn't get mad over it. She knew he was doing what he promised to do when he was a little lad. He was looking after her, and she loved him for that. Jack was a man of his word, and he made her feel safe. You would have to have a death wish, to pick a fight with Jack Malone. Jack was sitting in his room watching TV. He heard the front door slam and realised that prick that claimed to be his dad was home. It wasn't long until the shouting began. Jimmy was shouting at Irene. "Get up off of your fat, ugly fucking arse and make me some food." Irene instantly jumped up from the sofa. "Alright, alright, keep your fucking hair on." She walked into the small kitchen and instantly started frying bacon and eggs. Irene stood by the cooker and watched as the eggs cackled and the bacon sizzled.

In her mind she left the flat and was on a beach in some exotic country, with a cocktail and a big fuck off spiff in her mouth. Suddenly the smoke alarm went off, and Irene broke out of her dream. She pulled the pan away from the flame and swore out loud, "Shit, shit ,shit, for fuck sake." Jimmy came up behind her and pulled her head back by her hair. He got in her face as he said. "See what I mean? You fat ugly whore. You are fucking useless; you can't even fry a fucking egg you stupid cow! You need a lesson in fucking cooking." With that he grabbed her right hand and held it over the flame.

"Do you feel that? Do you?" "Please don't Jimmy, please! I'm sorry. I'm so sorry." "I don't fucking care about your pathetic fucking sorry's. You are a shit wife, a fucking good for nothing little trollop, who needs to learn a fucking lesson. Can you feel this bitch? "He pushed her hand in to the naked flame, and she let out an almighty scream.

The pain was intense and she withered and wriggled, trying to pull herself away to safety.

Irene ended up on the kitchen floor, sobbing with him standing over her. She looked up and couldn't believe what she saw. Jack had walked into the kitchen and grabbed his dad. "What you fucking playing at you little cunt." Jack didn't say anything. He didn't have to, as everything he needed to say was written all over his face. His veins were pulsing out of the side of his forehead. He grabbed his dad by the throat and shoved him up against the wall. The red mist washed over Jack, and he started smashing his dad's head against the wall.

Jack punched him hard in his face. And when Jimmy finally fell to the floor, he continued to kick him in his ribs. And he stamped on him with all of his weight. It wasn't until he heard Amy screaming that he stopped. "Jack stop! Jack Stop!" She pulled him away and looked into his face. " Jack its OK. I'm here. You have to stop." Jack was shaking with anger, and he was biting his tongue so hard that it was actually bleeding. He looked at Amy and instantly calmed down. "Are you OK Ames?"

"Yes. Yes, I'm fine." It was as she finished those words that Jimmy tried to get up. Jack quickly kicked him back down then dragged him up by his shirt. "Look at her. Fucking look at your daughter you dirty fucking scum." Jimmy's eyes wondered to the floor. "I said fucking look at her." Jimmy looked up and saw his daughter's big teary eyes, staring at him in disbelief. "That is the last fucking time you ever look at her. Do you understand cunt!"

Jimmy nodded and closed his eyes. "You go near her again, and I swear to you now I will fucking kill you! And I will fucking make sure you feel everything I do to you. From now on you don't fucking speak, until spoken to! Do you understand?" Jimmy couldn't believe what he was hearing. "But this is my house." "Not anymore it fucking ain't. You belong to me now. This is my fucking house. And if you put one foot out of place, I will fucking kill you."

They stared at each other, both wondering who would look away first. Jimmy couldn't help himself. He looked to the floor, beaten, bruised, and hurt. Not only had he never been beaten like this before, he had the shit kicked out of him by his own fucking son. The shame and embarrassment took over him. There he was sitting in the corner of his kitchen, actually crying big sobs. Amy picked up her mum and helped sooth her hand. It seemed like ages, since they were all stood in the kitchen in absolute silence. Irene told her daughter, "It's OK now Amy. It feels much better thank you." She wrapped her hand in a tea towel and walked over to her husband. Irene stared at him for what seemed like a lifetime, and then she spat in his face. Jimmy wanted to batter her, but he had no strength. He knew his legacy as leader of his family was over. Jimmy was simply weak, beaten, and shamed.

CHAPTER 2

The Rise of Jack

Amy got her first job at the local off license. Reggie the boss let Jack help out with the lifting and stacking of the shelves at weekends too. He watched Jack, as he lifted crate after crate and was amazed at his strength and energy. "You know Jack, you remind me of me when I was your age. I was a good looking lad built exactly like you. In fact I bet people would think we were brothers." Jack laughed. He really liked Reggie. Reggie was a real joker. He was good to his sister, and Jack respected him for that and was grateful. "You know Reggie, I hope I look just like you when I am 85." "You cheeky little shit. I'm nowhere near 80 fucking 5. You're not too big for a thick ear, you know lad?" Jack laughed again, and Reggie joined in. "Bloody 85 cheeky little fucker." With that Reggie passed Jack a beer, and they sat on a beer barrel drinking.

They would sit drinking and talking for hours. Reggie would tell him stories of when he was a lad, and he would listen to Jack too. Reggie gave good advice. He told Jack to stay away from the gang bangers and get a decent job, even if it wasn't completely legit. Reggie would tell him, "Don't go selling yourself short son." Jack always kept that advice in the back of head. As he thought to himself, it was the only intelligent thing Reggie had ever said. He would smile to himself whenever he thought of it. It didn't take long for Jack to get noticed by the local street gangs. They all wanted to recruit him, but he wasn't interested. He didn't give a fuck about turf wars and what tattoo meant what on your body. Jack wanted to be where the money was at, so he could provide for his sister. And they could get out of that shit hole they called home.

Jack got his first break at 17. He got a security job in a club, and he worked the door in the evenings. He had to sort out enough shit in the club. Jack was always seeing off wanna be bad boys and drunken hard men. He enjoyed his job and the respect that he eventually gained from real bad boys, not the local street gangs or the wanna be gangsters.

We are talking the big faces of London. His name soon got about, and it was Benny Dowling that took the initiative to recruit the young lad, as a personal minder. That was when he started making the real money. He looked up to Benny and watched closely at how he ran his business. Jack listened intently to his advice on everything and anything. Benny and Jack became great friends.

He trusted Jack with everything, from protecting his family from the gangsters he would rub up the wrong way, to protecting his many business empires. Benny owned strip clubs, casinos, and even a scrap yard. He was loaded, but money meant nothing to him. They would visit one of Benny's clubs regularly. It was called The Shady Nook, and Jack always thought that name suited the place. The walls were a purple colour, and there were chandeliers hanging from the ceiling. The floors were all wooden, and there was a big dance floor in the middle, which housed a couple of poles that the girls would gyrate around, wearing practically nothing.

This wasn't something that interested Jack. He didn't see how some naked chick with dyed hair, fake tits, and fake fucking eye lashes dancing around a fireman's pole was sexy. All the women fancied Jack though. It was obvious however Jack just simply wasn't interested. He preferred the sweet and innocent girls, the ones with real jobs and prospects. Jack liked ones that he had to teach how to be a whore in the bedroom. "Go on for fuck sake Jack. Will you take one of these hungry, horny little bitches and get your fucking end away?" "Don't start Benny. You know I don't do that." "Do what? Have fucking sex? Are you a virgin Jack? Is that what this is about?" "Fuck off Benny. You know I ain't no virgin. I just have standards that's all." "Did you hear that girls? Jack has standards, so you can stop thinking you're getting lucky."

Benny roared with laughter, and Jack just sat at the bar drinking his beer. He hated it when Benny was in one of these moods, because he always seemed to be the brunt of his fucking jokes. Jack always let it go though. If it wasn't for Benny, he would be broke and still living in that dump. They worked together for years, until Benny had a stroke. He lost the use of his left side, and that was when he had to retire. Jack still had his hand in everything, but he let Phillip, Benny's son, run the day-to-day business. He made sure that he had set him up with some good minders, and that he was capable of running Benny's empire. But without Benny Jack just simply didn't want to be that involved anymore. So he became the sleeping boss.

Jack was the brains and the real man in charge of all of Benny's gaffs, but Phillip became the face of it all. The new arrangement suited everyone, and he still kept in touch with Benny. Jack went over to watch the footy on occasions, but it broke his heart watching his friends face look so vacant, watching him struggle to speak, having to wear a bag to piss in. It was simply too much for Jack to take in. Benny was an empty shell. No one said that out loud, but everyone knew it. Benny had gone.

Jack saved every penny he earned and eventually managed to move him and Amy out of that rat-infested estate. He bought his first home aged 21. It was a three bed semi on the outskirts of London. He lived there with Amy for years, and they were the best years of his life. However time moves on and things change. Amy eventually got married and had kids. He gave her the house, which she later sold to buy a bigger place for her family.

Jack had a few properties, but the one he chose to live in was different. It was in the middle of nowhere. Hardly anyone knew it existed. It was surrounded by nothing but fields. The place had a long dirt track that led to the main road, but this track was hidden. No passer by would notice it. He had barns and outhouses. But apart from that, it was just green grass. It was the solitude that Jack loved about his house. He liked sitting in silence with his own thoughts. Jack had a TV and all the latest mod-cons, but they were mainly for show. He hardly ever used any of them. Silence was his best friend.

PART II

THE CONFESSIONS

CHAPTER 3

THE FIRST CONFESSION:

WHEN BOYS CRY

It was a sunny Monday afternoon, and Jack was thinking about the job he had completed last night and how he had refreshed his soul in the confession box. He enjoyed that part of his religion. Jack wasn't exactly a devout Catholic, and he didn't follow all of the rules. He didn't agree with not being able to have sex before marriage. When it came to abortion, Jack didn't agree that it was a complete sin to have an abortion. As far as he was concerned, some people shouldn't be parents. After some of the things he had witnessed, sometimes it was cruel for some people to give birth. Jack sat in the small snug confession box, waiting to be given the go ahead to speak. He knew as soon as father Patrick heard his voice, he dreaded what he was going hear.

But Jack made a healthy contribution to the

church fund after each confession, which made it worth his while. At first Father Patrick thought it was only right to listen to the sins of this child. It was only right to offer his hand of forgiveness, since he was at least aware that he had actually sinned. When Jack asked for forgiveness, in Father Patrick's eyes, that was a man who regretted his actions. He told himself his acceptance of this child's confession had nothing to do with the 30 grand that he would leave afterwards.

Jack started his confession with, "Forgive me father for I have sinned." Father Patrick didn't bother to read a passage from the Bible, as he knew this child of God wasn't truly interested. "It has been six months since my last confession." "Go ahead child; speak from your heart and soul. God is listening and is waiting to help unload your heavy shoulders." With that Jack proceeded to talk about last night's events. He always started with his reasoning behind his crime. Today in particular he talked about his childhood and his sister. Jack talked about how much he loved her and how he felt he needed to free Gods children, from the evil that existed in this mean world.

"My sister Amy was a good child. She had her whole life ahead of her, yet she was dealt such a roar deal from the moment she was born. She was delivered to an evil father, a father that beat and raped her; a father that terrified his children and his wife with every breath he took. I was young, and I couldn't help her Father Patrick. However I am a grown man now, and I protect her and my nephews and will do for as long as I live. I haven't had children myself Father, but I appreciate all of Gods children. They are after all born innocent. It is man that introduces them to evil. It is man that shows them right from wrong; it is man that allows them to live in poverty; and to be abused by society. I am a man who can and will make a stand for these children. I want to protect them from the evil people that exist in this world. I lay it to rest Father, so evil can no longer destroy God's work."

Father Patrick couldn't believe his ears. This person was talking like he was God's soldier. He believes that he was put on the earth to rid the world of evil, even though this so called Catholic child was also evil. But on this occasion he wouldn't judge, as the church needed this man's contribution more than any one of the parishioners realised. It was at times like this that Father Patrick wondered how Amy was so different to her brother. He knew that she took the brunt of their father's beatings. And if this confession was to be believed, she was also raped by the parent that should have showed her nothing but love. So why was she so pleasant, and this brother of hers had grown to be so angry and evil minded?

This man twisted God's words to suit his needs, to give him reasons to kill, and to make him feel better about his criminal activity. Father Patrick sighed a deep sigh. It was moments like these Father Patrick wondered if he was the right man for this job. He couldn't see the positives in sitting here, allowing this man to gloat about his violent murderous actions. However it was his job, and he had promised to do his best by God. So he listened with baited breath, as Jack told him every detail about his last killing.

Jack waited outside the flat that he had been watching on and off for weeks. Tonight was the night. He was in the mood for a good kill. After the day he had, this dickhead was going to get it big style. It was around 11.30 p.m., and thankfully the estate was beginning to quieten down. The teenage hood rats had moved on, and most of the flats had their lights out. This was a typical London council estate. The walls were full of graffiti. There was rubbish all over the place, and realistically no one who appreciated their life came out after 9:00 p.m. Trouble was rife, but Jack didn't give a shit about any of that. He was here for one reason and one reason only; he had a job to do. A job that in his mind only he was capable off.

Jack took a large sip out of the whiskey bottle that he kept in the glove box for nights like these. He clasped his rosary beads that hung from the rear-view mirror, silently blessed himself, and whispered a quick prayer. This was his ritual whenever he had a big job on or whenever he knew that he was about to sin. However Jack knew that he would be forgiven, because he was actually ridding the earth of evil. In his mind it was something that God would appreciate. He was looking out for the good people, and that was his duty to God. It was cold and dark, as most of the street lamps were broken. He laughed to himself as actually, the fact that the council hadn't fixed the night lamps was a blessing to him. Jack wondered for a moment at how the police expected to solve crimes, when it was so fucking easy to be a criminal. He found himself laughing out loud. Jack always had a rush of adrenalin before a big job.

This kind of job excited him. He was taking out a complete cunt, and the whole world should fucking thank him. Jack had been given this job by an old associate of his, and he did a lot of work for him in this kind of setting. He was the best contract killer around; all the big faces used him, when they had a legitimate reason to off someone. Jack didn't take just any job. He didn't get involved with turf wars or bollocks like that. In fact he would be insulted if any one asked him to. Jack got rid of the real scum. The paedophiles, the people smugglers, and so forth were his prey. His favourite type of job was this one. He enjoyed getting rid of the scum, the nonces that preyed on children. The more he thought about those poor little kiddies, the angrier he got.

He picked up his tool box from the passenger seat of his Focus. This was his work car. It wasn't too in-your-face to stand out. To be honest it could do with having a total re-spray. But for this kind of work, it was perfect. Jack got out of the car and took in the cold fresh air. What a great night to end a nonce's life. Jack walked up the pathway to the flat. He kicked the flimsy front door off with one big kick. He wasn't worried about the noise, because it was a regular occurrence in this neighbourhood. Darren woke up with a fright. He thought he heard something and could have sworn it was his door. Darren got up out of his bed and grabbed his baseball bat that he kept in the corner. His breathing was heavy, as he could hear footsteps throughout the flat.

At first he told himself to calm the fuck down. It was probably a practical joke or maybe he was dreaming. He decided to hide behind the open bedroom door. Darren looked through the crack of the door and could see a figure walking towards him. He was fucking massive, and Darren felt bile rise in his throat. What the fuck was some giant doing in his fucking yard? What the fuck was this about?

As Jack walked through the bedroom door, Darren shouted, "What the fuck do you think you're playing at in my house?" He raised the bat and tried to whack him with it. Jack caught the bat with one hand and pushed Darren up against the wall. He looked into his eyes and saw how scared he was, and that turned Jack on even more. He loved the look of fear. Jack laughed in his face so closely that Darren could feel his breath. He could smell the whiskey, and he suddenly realised this was real; he was in deep fucking shit. All he could think of was to try and reason with this lunatic.

Darren cried real wet tears streaming down his face. "Listen take what you want. I have money. You can take it all! Please don't do this. I swear this is a mistake. You have got the wrong man please." Jack smirked and replied, " Really? Surly you can do better than that! You aint talking to no five year old now you know. If you think you can talk your nasty perverted self out of this, then think again. I aint got no time for mummies' boys, so quit your fucking crying. Today is a special day for you, and do you know why? "No, please let me go." "I said quit the fucking whining. It's your special day, as it is your last fucking day alive. And I am going to have a great fucking time at this farewell party." With that Jack laughed a real belly laugh. Darren's face was a picture. He didn't know what to do with himself. Darren thought, "Surly this can't be happening. Surly this nutter aint for fucking real," but Jack chucked Darren on the bed with such force that he thought his back was broken. He lay there unable to move. Darren watched in absolute fear, as Jack opened up his toolbox.

The piss trickled down his leg, making his white pants turn yellow. Darren needed to get out of there. He needed to raise the alarm. Surely this wasn't the way he was going to die. Surely he deserved better than this, but Darren knew why Jack was there. "Listen mate. It aint what you think. You have got it all wrong. I don't touch the kids. In fact I look after them you know. It's a fucked up world we live in. I protect them from the real fucking monsters out there. No one dies. They are well paid, and I make sure nothing really bad happens to them you know, cause I care about them." "Are you having a fucking laugh you little cunt?" "No, no, I'm serious; I don't hurt them!" Jack grabbed both of Darren's hands and tied them together, with a small piece of rope.

Darren screamed and tried to fight back, moving his body as best he could to the other side of the bed, trying to escape this mad man. He didn't get far before Jack grabbed his legs and tied his feet together too. "Please mate listen. You don't have to do this. I promise I will stop." "I aint your fucking mate, When are you going to realise I don't fucking like you? I think you are scum. I want you to feel pain, real pain, just like those boys did, when you allowed them to be raped by your sick fucking mates." " No! They aint my mates. They made me do it, cause I owe them money. And they threatened to kill me if I didn't. Please man; you got to listen to me. None of this is down to me. None of this is my fault." " Well if that is really the case, you are going to wish you let them kill you, cause I can promise you; it would have been better than what I have got planned for you." Jack laughed again, as he stuffed Darren's mouth with cloth. He turned his back on the pathetic man and started to whistle, as he set out his weapons on the floor.

All Darren could do was lay there and cry silent

tears. He found himself looking around the bedroom and wondering how his life had ended up like this. How had he ended up in this shitty little flat? The wallpaper was ripped. The carpet was threadbare; the only good thing in the whole place was the TV. On the money he made, he should be living in a massive five-bed house, with a pool and stables for fuck sake. His problem was the coke and the gambling. He was a sucker for them both. Darren took the coke excessively. In fact you could say it was what he lived for. Lines of coke and a night at the local casino was Darren living the high life, and that really was as good as it got for him. It was only then, whilst laying on this bed, that he realised what a major fuck up his life was.

If only he could of kept the money he made; if only he wasn't so fucking weak. He suddenly realised "if only" was all he had left now. Darren wasn't going to walk away from this; he wasn't going to be able to fix his ways. This was how he was going to die, in his fucking pants, in this fucking dingy pokey little flat, in the middle of a run down, fucking council estate. Oh! His mum would be so fucking proud. He hated the fact that his bitch mother was right. She always said his life would result to nothing, and she was so fucking right. What a fucking waste. In his mind Darren was a good man. OK, he liked the younger lads, but hey that was just his preference. Darren didn't advertise the fact that his preference was slightly different, to other so-called normal folk.

He kept his business quiet and had a selected few clientele that used his services. Darren was sure they hadn't opened their trap. He provided a service, a service that no-one else could provide. How dare society tell people how to feel, what to like, and how to live their fucking lives? Anyway he saw that these kids were well rewarded for their time and efforts. It was only the other day that he brought some mouthy little fucker a BMX to keep him sweet.

Darren made shit loads of money. In his trade of little boys, he did try to expand to little girls once, but they were more hassle than they were worth. He got more money for boys, and they tended to keep their mouths shut. Girls were squealers and fucking cry-babies. He couldn't be doing with their crap. Anyway his preference was boys, and at least he could get first dibs on any fresh meat this way. That was how he eased the boys in gently, showing them how much he cared. As everything after that first time would be so much worse for them.

The sound of the chain saw broke Darren's chain of thought, and he suddenly started to literally shit himself. He knew this mad fucker meant business, and he knew he was well and truly dead fucking meat. Darren felt the tears stinging his eyes again, but he was unable to blink them away. He was unable to move at all and was literally frozen with fright.

Jack's voice was deep, and he got close to

Darren's face when he said, "Don't worry cunt. We will save the best part for last. I want you to experience every bit of my tool kit, starting with these." Jack held up some pliers and waved them in the air. He chuckled out loud and started humming a tune, as he grabbed Darren's left hand. He sang, "This little piggy went to market. This little piggy stayed at home, and this little piggy was a perverted little cunt, who rapes little boys. Say bye little piggy; you nasty piggy." With that he cut off a finger. The pain was excruciating. Darren tried to scream but couldn't, as his mouth was full of cloth. Jack started singing again, and Darren knew he was about to lose another finger. His silent tears ran fast down his cheeks, and when he felt the second finger get the chop, he passed out.

Jack was on a roll. It was at times like these he really appreciated his job. This little cunt was never going near a child again. Every time he thought of a child, it made him angrier, and Darren experienced that anger with another Sharp object. Darren was in and out of consciousness, but Jack made sure he woke him up for the good bits. I mean that was the least he could do. He made sure Darren knew he was going to lose those dirty, perverted little eyes of his. Jack even took the cloth out of his mouth, so he could hear him scream, whilst he gouged out his eyes with an ice pick. The whole time Jack laughed at this perverted sick individual. He took his time in everything he done. After all if a job is worth doing, it is worth doing well, and Jack always took pride in his work.

The grand finale in Jack's routine was to cut off his dirty little cock and stuff it in his big ugly mouth. Jack knew that he was dead by now, but he still took it upon himself to say out loud every move he was making; every cut he took pleasure in, just in case that little fucker hadn't taken his last breath yet.

For good measure Jack thought it was a good idea to cut the cunt's head off too. Show this motherfucker's family and friends that he was a proper nonce, filthier than any other filth on the streets. People like him deserved to be shamed; they deserved to be hurt; they deserved a date night with Jack Malone. He was glad that he saw to this particular nonce personally, and that he ended up where he should be, in the fucking toilet with the other filth and dirty fucking rats.

As Jack walked out of the flat with his tool bag, he looked around to make sure all was quiet. As he thought no one was around, and if anyone was about watching his every move, no one would talk. Even if they did, Jack didn't give a shit. He was proud of his night's work. As far as he was concerned, he had done the world a favour. He had given those kids justice, something that the pathetic pussy police couldn't ever do. Jack didn't believe them fuck wits couldn't even guarantee a prison sentence these fucking days.

The whole British justice system was a total

sham. He would get a bigger sentence for dealing drugs than raping some kid. Jack's reasoning behind this was that the police and magistrates were all fucking queers too, and they looked after their own. Seriously who would really trust someone that wore a fucking oversized cloak and a wig to work? What a fucking joke!

As Jack drove home, all he could think about was his bed. He wasn't getting any younger, and his job took it out of him these days. However he knew that the dude who sanctioned this death would be pleased with his work. Jack knew he would probably get a healthy bonus for his extra-special activity that evening. The thought of the money made Jack smile. He told himself that was why he done these jobs. Jack told himself he was delivering justice to those who deserved it most, and that he needed the money.

Truth was Jack was loaded. He didn't need any more money, and he took no less that £60.000 per contract. Obviously all that was tax-free and paid in cash. If Jack was truly honest with himself, he done this job because he needed the feeling he got, when he saw fear on another person's face. He loved the kill, and he loved the torture. Most of all Jack loved that his face was the last one that they saw, before they died. He didn't need the money, the big house and nice cars. All he needed was the thrill he got from helping to cleanse Gods Kingdom!

Detective Dan Pearce was sitting at his desk in the corner of the Murder Investigation Unit,

Scotland Yard. He took a large sip of his black coffee and looked down at the photographs in front of him. They were truly gruesome. This was no ordinary murder; this was some proper sick shit. In his whole career he had never seen anything like it. The victim's head had literally been severed off of his shoulders; his eyes had been gouged out; and his penis had been cut off and shoved in his mouth.

This was definitely a personal murder, but who would have the stomach to perform such acts, on another human being? Surely you would have to be some kind of bionic super human, to be able to pull off this psycho shit. He closed the folder quickly, as he felt the brandy he had last night slide back up his throat. Dan knew he shouldn't drink on the job, but after walking in to the murder scene, he needed something to take the edge off.

He arrived at the scene at around 4 a.m. Dan was called directly by the chief, which meant there was no time for fucking about. He knew he had to get there sharpish. As Dan arrived, so did his partner John. He looked as happy to be there as Dan. They nodded acknowledgment of each-other and silently walked up the concrete steps towards the flat.

The door had clearly been kicked off, and there was a young PC bent over outside the flat, throwing his guts up in a bin. The men looked at each other with an expression that showed both of their nerves. Dan stepped inside and met the chief standing in front of him. "Morning Chief. Would say nice to see you, but judging by your face, I'm not going to enjoy this little get together." "Don't joke Dan. This aint the fucking time for it."

Dan instantly felt embarrassed at his own lack of sensitivity. The chief had this way of making him feel two-feet-tall. "Get your arses in here and tell me what you think of this." Both Dan and John followed the chief in to what seemed to be the bedroom. Only this bedroom was different; this bedroom had blood up the walls. The bed was covered in blood and human excrement. The stench was enough to make anyone heave.

Dan and John instinctively put their hands over their mouths and noses, to try to mask the smell and disguise the urge they both had to throw up. It was like a horror movie scene. There was what looked to be a male body on the floor. The head had been removed. On closer inspection so had the fingers on the left hand, and both big toes. The amount of blood was surreal. John asked, "So where is the head?" The chief pointed to the bathroom. They all walked briskly out of the bedroom and slowly across the hall to the bathroom. Dan didn't want to go inside. Something in his gut told him not to look, but unfortunately for him he knew he had to.

He stepped inside the small bathroom, and straight ahead of him was the toilet. Only this toilet was different, because this toilet had a head popping out of the bowl. Dan looked and said,

"What the fuck! This is some fucked up shit John. Take a look." Dan turned his back to the toilet and ushered John forward. He watched the expression on John's face change, from intrigue to disgust in an instant. "For fuck sake, what the fuck is that?"

The chief was still standing in the hallway, knowing what was in the bathroom. He decided to stay there. The chief spoke in a low voice, "That is the victim's head." "Well fuck me Chief. I kind of guessed that myself, but what the fuck is that in his mouth? And where the fuck are his eyes?" "Well Sherlock, that is his penis hanging from his mouth, and we are yet to find his eyes." "Fuck me Dan. This can't be real; this guy wasn't murdered. He was fucking tortured. What the Fuck! "It certainly looks that way, but your job lads is to find out who, why, and how." With that the chief left. Dan looked at John in disbelief, and all he could say was, "I need a fucking drink."

CHAPTER 4

THE SECOND CONFESSION:

TAMING THE NURSE

Karen stood in the dock and stared at the jury. It was the first time that she felt nervous. She knew she hadn't slipped up in her perfect murders. In her head she didn't see them as proper murders. Old people were a strain on society, and they rarely wanted to live anyway. They had lived their lives. Old people were sick and frail; why would they want to live? It was the families that kept them going, and Karen thought those families were selfish. She was a nurse and worked in a NHS hospital. The last thing the NHS needed was the strain of paying the medical bills, of someone who was ready to die.

It pissed her off that she had to feed these people, take them to the toilet, clear up their shit and sick, and restrain them from hurting

themselves. That wasn't nursing; that wasn't what she signed up for. She wanted life and death situations. Therefore she created her own life and death situations. Karen decided who lived and who died. It was her ward, and she played God.

It made her feel great, especially when the family of the patient would thank her for her hard work. Unbeknown to them they were helping her kill their loved ones. The court usher broke her chain of thought. "Please rise." Everyone got to their feet. She put on her desperate innocent face just for the judge and jury. The court was seated, and Karen's palms began to sweat. The judge said, "Will the foreman of the jury please stand. Have the jury reached a verdict in all eight counts of murder." "Yes we have." "In the case of Edith Jones, do you find the defendant guilty or not guilty?" "We the jury find the defendant not guilty." This was the verdict of all eight counts. Karen couldn't believe her luck. She knew she was good, but even she couldn't believe she got away with everything. Detective Dan looked at his partner opened mouthed.

They couldn't believe what they were hearing. This bitch killed eight people, whilst pretending to be someone that cared for them. They knew that the chief wasn't going to be happy about the verdict. Not only had they got nowhere with the torture murder in Brixton, but this case was supposed to be a no brainer. No ward loses eight patients under the care of the same nurse, in 12 months all in the same way. This is what they called an open and shut case. The verdict couldn't be not guilty. The chief definitely wasn't going to be happy.

Karen waited for at least a couple of hours, before she left the courthouse without being detected by the families of the deceased and the paparazzi. She got on a train and left London as soon as she could. Karen wore a woolly hat, a long coat, and glasses to disguise herself from the public. She knew her face had been all over the local news and papers, and the last thing she needed was agro from the average wannabe hero. She made her way to Milton Keynes. It wasn't too far from London, but she felt it was far enough.

She asked the taxi man to take her to a local B&B and proceeded with the transformation from Karen Johnson, suspected killer, to Joyce Jones, nurse, carer, grandma and all round nice person. She dyed her hair grey and cut it dead short. Joyce added glasses and blue contact lenses to her new look and couldn't believe how different she looked. Her fake ID was excellent and well worth the £500 she paid. This was it; this was the new and improved pensioner, Killer Joyce. She was back and back with vengeance.

It was easy getting a job at the local hospital, as they were crying out for nurses, especially ones that preferred working with the elderly. Joyce went into work with a smile on her a face and a spring in her step. Everyone instantly liked her. She offered to do the shitty jobs that everyone hated, and that went down well. However the rest of the staff didn't know that she also hated those shitty jobs.

Joyce hated feeding, washing, protecting, and cleaning up the shit of those that could no longer care for themselves. How fucking degrading and pointless. Arnold was 82. He had dementia and was currently admitted to the hospital with a chest infection. Joyce could tell he had given up on life, just by looking at his bony shell of what used to be a healthy male. "Good morning Arnie, my love. Are you hungry?"

Arnold looked at Karen like she had asked him the final question in, "Who Wants to be a Millionaire." What do you mean am I hungry? Bloody hell woman, I've just eaten." "No, you haven't Arnie. That was yesterday. It is 8 a.m. now, and you need some breakfast. Now are you going to be good today and eat it all up?" "Why are you talking to me like that? I am not bloody five you know. I have fought in the bloody war." "Yes, so you keep telling me, and what a great job you done. I bet you looked handsome in your uniform."

"Well yes, I did. I will have you know that I had the girls fighting over me back then." "I bet you did Arnie. Now here you go. Open wide and show me what a soldier you can be with your breakfast." Joyce didn't wait for a reply. As soon as he opened his mouth slightly, she shoved the spoon in.

Breakfast for Arnold this morning was Weetabix laced with skimmed milk and antifreeze. That was just what the doctor ordered and just what Arnold needed to get himself on the road, to his next life. That is what she told herself anyway. Joyce made sure Arnold had every mouthful. She also made him a cup of tea also laced with antifreeze.

Arnold's wife came in just after breakfast. Annie hated seeing her husband like this, but she knew that he was in the right place. Arnold's new nurse was wonderful. She couldn't believe how much attention she gave him and her for that matter. Annie sat watching her husband sleep, when Joyce interrupted her thoughts by saying, "Good morning." "Oh, hello Joyce. Sorry, I was in a world of my own then." "It's fine my lovely, but I have to say that you are looking awfully tired. Are you looking after yourself properly?" "Yes, of course I am." "Well you know Arnie is my priority right now. After all he is the sick one." "That may be Annie my love, but he needs you to be fighting fit to help him pull through." "Pull through? You make it sound like he is going to die. He only has a chest infection"

"Yes, I know that, but he isn't as young as he used to be. And his body takes longer to recover from these episodes of ill health." "Yes, I know. I actually thought to myself when I walked in, he looks no better." "He is in the best possible hands Annie. You can be sure of that." "Oh, I know that, and I can't thank you enough Joyce for everything you and the staff are doing for him." "No need to thank me. It's just my job, and I love it. Between you and me Arnie is one of my special patients. I enjoy looking after him. It is my absolute pleasure." "I am so grateful. I can finally rest easier knowing he has you looking out for him." "That's why you should go home and rest more. After all as you said he has me, and I will make sure he gets everything he needs. I will also make sure he rests too." "Maybe you are right. I am feeling a bit tired. I could come back this evening." "Good idea. Go and rest or go shopping or something. Take advantage of having some you time. He will be safe in my hands." Joyce passed Annie her handbag and ushered her off of the ward. "Go on. I insist, off you go." "OK, I will be back later, and you will tell him that won't you?" "Of course."

Joyce watched Annie leave and smirked to herself. She knew thanks to her it wouldn't be long, until Arnold was in his final resting place. She would no longer have to listen to his crap war stories and tales of his childhood. If she was honest, that was what she really hated, especially patients with dementia. They talked all day about 50 years ago but couldn't remember their arse to their elbow. It was so bloody annoying. She didn't give a shit about their past. All she cared about was making sure they didn't have a fucking future. Joyce knew in her head that she was doing the right thing, by helping them on their way to the next life. Why would anyone want to stay alive without all of their faculties? Why would anyone want to carry on living without being able to walk properly, feed themselves, or use a proper toilet? It made no sense to her. More to the point it made no sense that the taxpayer was paying to keep them alive, and people like her had to clean up their shit and sick for fucking peanuts. It was a disgrace.

Joyce grabbed her jacket and went outside for a cigarette. It had been a pig of a day, and she had found it quite difficult to keep Arnold topped up with the antifreeze. Tomorrow she was going to suggest he goes on a drip, as that would make it so much easier. Joyce was standing in the alley and darkness had already fallen. She had worked a double shift, just to ensure that she could keep an eye on Arnold. Joyce placed the cigarette between her lips and looked in her pocket for her lighter. "Shit!" She realised it wasn't there. "Do you want a light love?" She turned around to see a handsome man holding out a lighter to her. "Cheers mate. I left mine upstairs." "No problem." As she bent her head forward to accept the light for her much needed cigarette, Jack grabbed her hair and smashed her head into the brick wall. She was so shocked that she didn't even scream. He smacked her head until she fell unconscious. Jack then dragged her to his car, which was parked close by. Then he stuck her quickly and efficiently into his boot.

If Jack was honest, he was shocked when he

got this job. The bitch had been all over the news, for killing the old folks that she was supposed to look after. He had caught bits of it on the radio, whilst relaxing in his garden. Jack wasn't one for TV. He watched it sometimes but only really for researching his new target or when he had visitors. Jack couldn't understand the fascination in TV. It was full of shit, and he would much rather listen to music or sit in silence with his own thoughts. Joyce woke up and realised she was in the boot of a car. The first thing that sprung to mind was a revenge attack from one of her victims' family. That thought instantly pissed her off. She was convinced no one recognised her, and that her ID was fool proof. Maybe she got followed from the court. Maybe some fucking lunatic was tagging her the whole time.

Great! This was all she needed. Not only was she in the middle of her first kill for over a year, but she was now in a compromising position, which she had to get out of. Joyce knew no one saw her down the alley, apart from the prick that assaulted her of course. She knew she had to think of something and quickly. Joyce was determined that this wasn't the way she was going to die. She would die when she fucking said so. That is what she does. She deals with life and death on a daily basis. Jack was driving his Ford Focus at a steady pace. He wasn't going to get pulled over by the police, with a body in his boot; he never took any chances like that. His favourite CD was playing, which always put him in a good mood and warmed him up for whatever the night entailed. It was Queen. He loved that band and especially loved Freddie Mercury. Jack loved his energy and the way he didn't give a fuck, about what anyone thought of him.

Obviously Freddie was dead now, but he was still a legend. He found himself singing along, which helped drown the kicking and shouting coming from the boot. Jack was shocked she was conscious so quickly. He pulled over on the hard shoulder and decided to shut her up. Jack opened the boot and punched her full in the face. She was petrified, and that just pleased Jack even more. "Shut the fuck up!" Joyce was silently crying and trying to steady her breathing. Jack stuffed cloth in her mouth and tied her hands and feet. That would shut her up. He looked in her eyes just before he closed the boot and said, "Get some sleep. We have a busy night ahead." Jack slammed the boot and laughed to himself, as he got back in to the car to resume the journey. Rita was wondering where the hell Joyce had gone. It really wound her up, when nurses took on double shifts and then done a disappearing act halfway through. She sent Dan one of the porters to go and look for her, but she wasn't holding her breath. Little did she know that Joyce was in the back of Jack's boot.

Jack stopped at the gates of the scrapyard. He had brought this place off of Benny a few years back. Jack needed to justify his assets, if he was ever asked. He saw this as a great cover, and he had made sure the place was going to be empty before he got there. The two Rottweiler dogs were going crazy at the sound of Jack's car. They looked really viscous when they barked and jumped about with white saliva dripping from their mouths. The fact was the dogs were soft as shit but clever. They did their job well. The dogs would attack if told to, and they would do a great job too. They certainly made intruders think twice. The Rottweilers also loved a fuss and playing fetch, not that Jack would let people see that side of them. He unlocked the gates and shouted for the dogs to shut up. Then Jack drove the car in to the yard and parked it right at the back. He opened the car boot and looked at Joyce. She had pissed herself, and Jack laughed at her. "What's up Karen? Couldn't you control your bladder?"

She looked at him, and her eyes widened. Karen couldn't believe he knew who she was. He took the cloth out of her mouth, and she instantly took her chance to talk her way out of her situation. "Who is Karen? You have got the wrong woman. My name is Joyce. You are making a mistake. Ask anyone." Jack roared with laughter. "How about I ask them old folks that you look after? Oh no! I forgot they are dead. So not saying much are they Karen? Don't make the mistake of taking me for a fool. I know who you are, so shut the fuck up." "No seriously, you have got it all wrong." "I said shut the fuck up!" With that he took the rag doused in chloroform out of the plastic bag and shoved it over her nose and mouth. She instantly relaxed and fell unconscious. Jack was relieved. He couldn't stand winging fucking woman.

They were the worst. He picked her up and tied her to a chair that he had already placed earlier that evening. Her head flopped to one side, and he couldn't help but smirk to himself. He would have a quick break, go for a piss, and fuss the dogs for a bit. Then he would wake that bitch up. Jack took a long drink from his whiskey bottle and held his rosary beads in his right hand.

He whispered a quick prayer and instantly felt ready to put this bitch to sleep, permanently. Jack opened a water bottle and added the Rohypnol. He wanted this bitch to be able to feel everything but be able to stop nothing. Karen started to wake up in the chair, and Jack gave her a helping hand, by chucking a bucket of water over her head. She choked and spluttered. And as Karen opened her eyes, she remembered the shit situation she was in.

"Drink this!" Without waiting for a reply, Jack forced the bottle in her mouth and enjoyed watching her choke, gulp and splutter. Once empty, he chucked the bottle to the ground and slapped her hard around her face. She yelped with shock. "Please stop this! I swear you have got your wires crossed. I am a good nurse. I help people." "Really? How is that? All you do is kill them. You watch as they suffer. You smile in the faces of their family, whilst you secretly kill their loved ones. You are no nurse."

Karen decided this had gone on way too long. She had been slapped, punched and shoved in the boot of the car. This man was taking the fucking piss. "Listen. Yes, I kill them, but I do it for them. I hate to see them suffering. All their families want to do is pump them with drugs, to keep them alive. It's not right. I help them on their way to their next life. They ask for my help. I give them the gift of peace, the gift of heaven. That is what they desire."

Jack laughed out loud. OK. Well if that is the case, why is it these people are admitted with only minor illnesses? But according to you they want to die. I told you before don't fucking bullshit me." Karen wanted to shout at him; she wanted to call him a prick and tell him about himself; she wanted to move; she wanted to straighten her head; she wanted to defend herself; but she couldn't. Karen suddenly felt really drunk and disorientated. In her mind she was screaming abuse, telling this fucking arsehole to let her go. But her body didn't move; her mouth didn't let out any sound.

All she could focus on was the face and the smile of the man, which she now knew was going to kill her. Jack untied her, as he knew the drug had kicked in. As she lay on the mud looking dazed and confused with glazed eyes, he kicked her in her ribs. She felt the pain of his hard kick but couldn't react. All she could do was watch as he prepped the machine. Karen didn't know what the machine done, but she knew she wasn't going to like this.

He picked her up and chucked her forcefully back in to the boot of his car. Jack parked the car in to position. He opened the boot and smiled as he said, "Time for you to meet your destiny and for me to get a new car." Jack laughed loudly, as he slammed the boot shut. He manoeuvred the machine and picked up the car with its crane. Karen knew she was in mid-air, but she still couldn't function. The noise was horrific, and she realised even if she could scream, no one would be able to hear her.

She knew this was her last living moment, and all Karen could think about was the fact she didn't get finished with Arnold. She was pissed off about that, and she was also pissed off that this was her ending. Silent tears fell down her cheeks, and Karen decided to close her eyes and wait for death to take her. There was nothing she could do. This was how she would die, at the hands of some nobody. Her last thought was that she wished she had gone to prison. Then Karen felt the car getting smaller and the frame of it getting closer. She knew then she was to be crushed, and finally she was able to scream. She felt her legs break and her knees pop out of the skin. Her arms snapped, and her ribs literally crumbled under the force of the crushing metal. Karen's eyes were forced out of her head, and her skull was crunched in to bits.

Jack laughed as he watched the windows of

the car smash and the body of the car crunch. He thought, "What a way to go." The best part of it was he didn't have to clean up. He needed a new car anyway and was glad he could kill two birds with one stone. Jack turned off the machine and walked towards his new car. He had ordered this in advance, and as usual it wasn't registered in his name. Jack never used his real name for any of his vehicles, but he always had decent ID to show, if he was ever questioned. He was proud of the way he left no paper trail behind him.

Jack decided to upgrade his work car this time to a Jeep. It had more room and was better to drive off road with when needed. His personal car was a Mercedes, and he loved that. But it wasn't practical for the jobs he needed to do. He tied his rosary beads to the rear view mirror. Jack enjoyed the smell of the new leather interior and relaxed in the heated seat, as he drove out of the yard listening to Queen. He was happy with a job well done!

Meanwhile, Father Patrick listened as Bishop Adam praised his fundraising skills. "I mean it Patrick. Your parish has made more money than all the others in our area. You must be so proud of your parishioners. They must have baked some great cakes." With that Adam laughed. He thought he was really funny. "What's the matter with you Patrick? You look so sad, and I am praising your good work. It is clear that the folk around here think a lot of you."

"Actually Bishop, I tend to disagree. I have one

parishioner that makes big donations to the church." "Well thank the Lord for him and his good will gestures Patrick." "You don't understand. The man comes to confession every now and again and leaves the money behind him." "That's great Patrick." " No. It isn't great. He tells me the most terrible things."

"Can I stop you there Patrick? You know as well as I do that people come here to confess their sins. It is not up to you or I to judge them. Only the Lord can judge, and that he will Patrick, when he sees fit. For the moment God has led this person to you. He has led him here to his house and has given him the chance, to cleanse himself and appreciate the Lord's words. It is up to you to show him the way Patrick. Don't judge his sins. That is not your job. Just listen and let him lean on you. He will find his way with your help." "No he won't. He is an evil man."

"An evil man doesn't seek forgiveness Patrick. An evil man doesn't give so handsomely towards the Lord's house and the Lord's followers. Now that would be damn right ridiculous. Don't you think?" "He confesses and leaves the money to make him feel better. That isn't right Bishop" "Why is that not right Patrick? All he is doing is thanking you for your services. What is wrong with that? If you are having trouble with the responsibilities of your calling Patrick, maybe we should talk on a more serious note. Maybe we should talk about whether you are capable of listening, without judging. As that isn't a good thing."

Patrick knew that was the Bishop's way of threatening him with losing his job, but he certainly couldn't say that out loud. It was clear to him that money talked, even in the eyes of the church. "No, Don't worry about me Bishop. I am as dedicated to my job as ever, and I won't let you or my community down."

"That's more like it Father Patrick. You are doing a great job, and if you continue to give your time to this troubled person, I expect to see more very generous donations. And that is only good for us Patrick. Remember that." "Absolutely. I will remember that." "Excellent! I am glad we have had this chat. I will leave you to get on. I notice a gentleman waiting for confession, so I won't keep you." Father Patrick looked around to see Jack sitting, waiting patiently for him to become free. He felt a shiver run up his spine and instantly regretted airing his concerns to the Bishop. What if Jack heard him? What if he was next?

Father Patrick watched Jack get up and move towards the confession cubical. Father Patrick couldn't move for at least a minute. Then he thought to himself, "This man, this human being is only a mere mortal." Unlike him he has God on his side, and that was the best protection any man could have.

He took a deep breath and told himself to do as he had promised his church and his parishioners. Father Patrick would listen and try his hardest not to judge. He will not however guide this troubled soul, as Father Patrick knew only too well it was too late for this individual. He was clearly a wicked and evil soul. However the thing that troubled him the most was what will happen when this man realises there is no good inside of him, and he wasn't actually doing God's work? What will happen when this troubled person kills for fun, rather than redemption? He won't be able to justify that as God's work.

At the moment his victims have all been evil souls, but inevitably this man will turn to kill for fun. Father Patrick decided there and then, on the spot, that this is when he will turn him away. For now he will just listen and accept his confessions and donations to the church, for the good of his people, as the Bishop said. As usual Father Patrick started with a prayer and asked Jack how long it had been since his last confession.

"It has been three months since my last confession." "Very well, release your sins." "Well Father as you know, I am a busy man ridding God's Kingdom of evil." Jack paused expecting Father Patrick to agree, but instead it went silent. "You may have seen on the TV Father about the old folks being killed off, in a hospital by a nurse." "Yes. I have seen that on the news, but I also saw that the lady in question was found not guilty."

"You are correct Father. In the eyes of the law, she was found not guilty. But in the eyes of the Lord, she was guilty as hell." "How is it you know this?" "Let's just say I have access to certain confidential information, so I know the truth. Also in this case when I met up with the lady in question, she admitted what she done. However she tried to talk her way out of it. Made out she was doing good by killing them off, but we know different to that Father. They were good people, law abiding citizens. And they had good families; they didn't deserve to die." "The Lord decides who lives and who dies. It is not for us to make decisions like that."

"What are you saying Father? That I am wrong to do God's work, to rid the world of these evil people? Is that what you are saying?" Father Patrick suddenly became nervous. If he was to be honest, he may be the next victim or he would no longer get the donations that the Bishop clearly stated were needed and lose his job. Either way, Patrick was in a situation he would rather not be in. "It is not I that can judge you. That is God's job."

Jack stayed silent for a while, which made Father Patrick more nervous. "Well Father, when you decided to go into the church, you had a calling from God right?" "Yes. That is correct." "Well when I was a youngster, I too had that calling, but God called on me to be His soldier. He called on you to spread His word, and He called on me to help Him fight the devil. Do you understand Father?" Father Patrick understood that this is what this delusional man thought, but he knew God only done good.

"I believe that you believe you had that calling,

and as I said before, I am not here to tell you that you are a liar or judge you for your actions. So please, continue." "To be honest with you FATHER, I have gone off of the idea of confessing my good work to you. As I feel you are judging me, and I feel that you may be jealous that God trusts me with the more dangerous work, rather than you." "That is absolute nonsense. I am not jealous of your so-called calling. I am just trying to fulfil my promises to God."

Again silence fell, and both men felt awkward. "Well I completed the job. She is gone and will no longer be killing innocent old folks, and that is about it really I suppose. That is all I need to say." "Excellent. I am glad you have aired your confession, and I hope you feel better in doing so. But can I ask you is there any point in me, asking you to say any Hail Mary's or for me to try and change your actions in the future?" "No Father. I don't believe there is. As I have done no wrong." "Well let's not continue this further. May God bless you."

With that Father Patrick got up and left. He went to his office and prayed; he prayed for forgiveness for accepting this man's confession, for knowing the evil soul that he is and doing nothing about it. Jack smiled to himself. He actually couldn't believe the way that the Father had just spoken to him. Who did he think he was? He was lucky that he is a holy man. Otherwise Jack would have taken serious offence to his actions, but as usual Jack left a hefty donation and made his way home, feeling lighter and cleansed.

CHAPTER 5

THE THIRD CONFESSION:

IF THESE WALLS HAD EYES

Jack got home from church in good time. He was still thinking about the sheer rudeness of that priest and decided he would leave less money at his next confession. Father Patrick might be a holy man, but he was also an arsehole. Jack didn't take too kindly to arseholes. His thoughts were interrupted by the phone. "Hello?" "Yeah Jack? It's me. I've got a new job for you. Can we meet? Shall we say in about an hour at Lola's café?" "Yeah, sure see you then." Jack instantly put his business brain in working mode. He wondered what this job was and thought to himself that God was clearly happy with his work, because straight after confession he got another job. Jack laughed to himself as he wondered, what that fucking Father Patrick would make of that. Lola's café was down a side street in Brixton. Jack always caught the tubes, when he was visiting Lola's to meet his boss, so that no one could track him. He knew that no one was following him. Even if they were, once they saw his boss, they would certainly look the other way.

Jack entered the café and kissed Lola on the cheek. She had owned this place for years and always welcomed Jack with open arms. "Hey gorgeous! How you doing?" She said with a wide grin. "I'm all the better for seeing you Lola." She laughed and instantly blushed. "If only that was true and if only I was 30 years younger, I would bite your hand off. You fancy your usual?" "That's my girl, always knows what I want. Yes. Please babe, I will have the usual, and I'm going to tuck myself up in the back corner. I got a bit of business. Make sure I'm not disturbed please love." With that he winked at Lola and handed her £300. She smiled and quickly stuffed the cash in her apron. "Righto my lovely." Lola busied herself making tea, whilst Jack got comfy in the back corner. He knew he could count on Lola's silence. That's the main reason he used this gaff. She was old school; she saw and heard nothing. He always dropped her a couple of hundred quid on every visit, and that was good enough for her.

Jack sipped his sugary tea and watched the steady stream of customers, as they went about their daily lives. No one took any notice of him, and he loved that. Lola had a mixed clientele from builders to hookers. They all ended up at Lola's café for a cheap cuppa and a bacon sandwich. Lola made conversation with them all. She didn't judge the hookers and certainly didn't rush them to leave. Unlike most of the café's around there, Lola accepted everyone and judged no one. She often found herself playing agony aunt to distraught girls, who had man trouble or bored husbands who had marriage trouble. That was the reason Lola loved her job so much.

Jack looked up and nodded his head at his boss, as he walked over and sat down. "Alright Jack?" "Yeah. I'm good, but something tells me that you're not. You look like a smacked arse. What's up?" Paul took a sip of his tea, which was already waiting on the table for him. "To be honest I feel like shit. I ain't slept properly for weeks, and now I have come to the conclusion that you are the only one who can help." "That's what I am here for." "Listen Jack, I ain't used to jobs that I give you being so close to home, if you know what I mean. So I am telling you straight. Don't fuck this up." "Did you just say don't fuck this up?" Jack was instantly offended. "Since when have I ever fucked anything up? You ain't talking to some drugged-up wannabe fucking gangster mate. So if you don't like my work, you know what you can do. Remember you need me. It ain't the other fucking way around."

Paul knew he had spoken out of turn and actually felt bad about it. He knew Jack was the best, and he also knew Jack was particular about all of his jobs and never fucked up. "I'm sorry Jack. I didn't mean it like that. My head is all over the fucking place. And like I said, I ain't slept. Don't take offence to anything I say. I am not myself."

Jack became intrigued and had already noticed something was really up with his usually cool, calm and shroud boss. "Alright, alright, apology accepted. Now will you tell me what the fuck is up with you?" "It's my girl. You know my daughter Jane. I think that lowlife scum husband of hers is kicking her about. Well in fact I know so." "OK, and?"

"What do you mean and? That's my fucking little girl Jack. I went round there the other month, and she had two black eyes and a fucking fat lip. She looked like something out of a horror fucking movie. I mean I asked her straight out if it was that fucking lowlife, and she said she had fell down the stairs. She blatantly lied for him Jack, to me her old dad. So when she was out and her house was empty, I had some cameras fitted in the lights. Fucking best thing I done. They aren't visible to the naked eye, but I get a live stream straight to my laptop. And she knows nothing about it"

"Cameras? Don't you think that is a bit over the top?" "Over the top? Are you having a fucking laugh? I mean at first I felt a bit guilty, but now I know it was justified. She hardly ever comes round anymore. She changes her plans to see us at the drop of a fucking hat, and now I know why. I thought it was cause she couldn't be arsed to listen to her mother chat shit about all the fucking neighbours, but now I have realised he has her

CONFESSIONS OF A CONTRACT KILLER

under his fucking thumb. She is shit scared of her own fucking shadow, and I for one ain't fucking having it." Jack had never seen his boss so angry. His veins were bulging at the side of his head, and his eyes were near to bursting with anger. "So why not deal with him yourself? I mean she is your daughter."

"Don't you see that is what I am doing? I can't go to the fucking police and have him arrested. I mean she will defend him, and how will that look to the outside world hey? I would never live it down. No this has to be sorted Jack. I'm not fucking having it. I want that cunt dead"

Jack knew he was being serious, and he knew that he would be the same if anyone laid a finger on his Amy. So he understood how he felt, and he actually felt sorry for him. But he had the feeling there was more to this story. "Alright, I get your pissed off cause he has hit your girl, but does that really warrant a death wish? Wouldn't you rather me just paralyse the cunt?" "No Jack. I want him dead. You will understand when I tell you this?" Jack looked at his boss and said, "Go on. I want to know everything."

"Right, well a while back our Jane came to see us and was the happiest I had ever seen her. She was with that twat, and I was always nice to him, even though I couldn't stand the little fucker ever since I met him. Anyway she tells us that she is pregnant, three months gone. She was delighted and so was her mother, and I'm not going to lie. I was proud as punch. I liked the idea of being a granddad. We celebrated, and I sat and listened to her chat about names and crap like that to her mother, for over an hour. Only the pregnancy didn't last Jack. She told us she had a miscarriage. We were devastated for her, and she was absolutely crushed Jack. It broke my heart to see her like that. She told us she fell off a horse, and that was how she lost the baby. I know she loves riding, but she is really good at riding horses. She has won trophies and all sorts. I thought at the time it was odd that she fell. I just had this feeling that she was covering something up. So I decided to go through the recent footage. I hadn't done that for a while. As to be honest it felt a bit weird watching my daughter go about her daily living. And to be totally honest I hadn't really seen anything to justify me watching. But I went with my gut and watched days' worth of footage. I could tell you what I saw Jack, but I don't want to down play it. I want you to see for yourself, so I have brought it with me"

Paul took out his laptop, set it up, and placed it on the table in front of Jack. Jack didn't say anything. He just put the earphones in and pressed play. Jane was busy in her kitchen making dinner for her husband Les, and Jack thought how happy she looked. He could hear her talking to her husband about the baby and could tell she was literally bouncing off of cloud nine. Jack looked at Les and could see he wasn't as happy. He was watching her like he hated her. His eyes were cold, and his face was like stone. Jane was totally oblivious to it all. She plated up her husband's dinner and laid it out in front of him. Les looked down at his plate of food. That is when it kicked off.

"Why don't you for once shut the fuck up?" Jane stood still and stopped dead in her tracks. "Look at this. Look at what you have given me to eat. Go on. Just fucking look at the state of it." Jane turned around slowly, and Jack could see she was shitting herself. "I'm sorry Les. I thought spaghetti was your favourite." "Are you telling me what I like and what I don't like now? Are you trying to say that you know me better than I know myself?" Jayne dropped her head and stared at the floor. "I'm sorry Les. I will make you something else." "Oh you will, will you? I don't fucking think so, you lazy fat fucking whore. I wouldn't eat anything you cooked for me right now, cause your ugly fucking face and your squeaky fucking voice has made me lose my appetite." "I'm sorry. Really, I am."

"You're having my baby, and this is what you call good fucking cooking? You ain't fit to be a mother Jane, and you certainly ain't fit to call yourself mother to my fucking child. "I'm sorry. I will get bet better. I promise I will do anything." She was crying now, and Jack could see that Les enjoyed upsetting her. Jane looked up at her husband, and he punched her full in the face. She screamed out in pain. He dragged her by her hair, sat her on his chair, and shoved her face in the dinner she had made for him. All the time he was calling her a useless ugly slag, slut, and ugly whore.

He pulled her head out of the plate and grabbed a knife from the table. He pulled her head back and put the knife to her throat. "Now tell me you little slut. Why I shouldn't kill you right now?" Jayne was uncontrollably crying. Blood was pouring from her busted nose, and she had food all over her face. "Please Les, I'm pregnant please!" "Oh yeah, so you are." With that he put the knife down and booted her off of the chair, so that she fell flat on her back. "Les no. Please don't, the baby!"

"It's my fucking baby you cunt, and I say you ain't fucking worthy of it!" With that Les stamped hard on her belly, continued to stamp and kick her in the stomach, and in between her legs all the while shouting, "Cunt! Cunt! Cunt! Cunt!" Jane curled up in the foetal position and held her stomach, as if to protect her child. So he stamped on her head instead. Jane fell unconscious and that infuriated Les. He wasn't finished yet.

Les kicked her some more. Then he filled the washing up bowl with cold water and chucked it over her face. She sputtered and choked, and he chucked the plate of food at the wall. "Now clean this fucking shit hole up. You are a fucking disgrace." Les walked out of the front door and slammed it behind him. Jane lay on the floor for ages, cradling her stomach and crying her eyes out. Eventually she stood up, and that is when Jack saw the blood flowing down her legs.

She was sobbing and openly praying to God to save her baby. Jack had seen enough. He closed the laptop and looked up at Paul. The men sat in silence for what felt like a lifetime. Jack really didn't know what to say. Paul looked at him and said, "Do you see why I need him dead? He is going to kill her Jack. To this day she sticks up for him and puts on a happy face in front of us, like they are the fucking Brady bunch. But I and now you know the truth, and I can't let that cunt kill my baby" "Did she go to the hospital?"

"Yes. She went by herself. I looked at her medical records. It seems that she falls over and has accidents a lot Jack, at least every six weeks according to her records. Now I know she wasn't born with two left fucking feet. I know that these falls only started shortly after she got hitched to that fucking dickhead. I looked up her notes for the time of the miscarriage, and guess what the doctor suspected? She had been attacked. She tried to convince her to go to the police, but Jane wouldn't hear of it. She even offered her some victim support and the details of a woman's refuge. A woman's fucking refuge! The clinical examination of her body that day showed what could be interpreted as a shoe print on her abdomen, a fucking shoe print for fuck sake. Don't you see he kicked my grandchild to death? He killed his own fucking child Jack, and I can't fucking have that. Do you understand?"

Jack nodded his head. He had heard enough; he wanted that little fucker's blood on his hands now. A husband and wife domestic is one thing, but stamping on a pregnant woman to kill a child is fucking sick. "The other thing I read in her notes was that it would be impossible for her to carry a child now. He has brutalised her that bad that she will never be able to be a mother. I think it is that knowledge that kills me the most." Jack finished his tea in silence then placed his cup back on the table.

He looked Paul in the eyes and he said, "Consider him dead." With that Paul got up and left. Jack sat for a while longer and went over the photos Paul had left of his daughter. She was a real beauty, blonde hair, green eyes, slim build and a smile that would light up any room. He recognised her but couldn't put his finger on where he had seen her. Then he saw the pictures from the hospital. Paul was right. She looked like she belonged in a horror movie. Her face was so black and blue you couldn't make out it was her. Even her hair was red with soaked blood.

There was no doubt in Jack's mind that this sick fuck was going to kill her in the end. He packed Paul's laptop and the photographs in to his brief case and left the café. Jack had a lot of planning to do because this was personal. He had actually witnessed the actions of this cunt, and Jack was going to torture him and enjoy every minute of it. Darkness had already fallen when Jack finally pulled himself up from his garden chair. He had sat in silence for hours, just going over everything that he had seen on that laptop. His thoughts turned to his childhood. He thought about his sister and the things he saw happen to her when they were young.

This overwhelming feeling of guilt came over him, and that soon turned to anger. He felt guilty that his big sister took his punishment. That his sister protected him from their dad, even though that meant she endured excruciating pain, pain that no one could take from her or heel for her. He protected her as best as he could when he realised what was happening, but he never really forgave himself for not putting his dad in a grave.

He went inside and poured himself a large whiskey. He sat at his kitchen table, whirling the whiskey around in his glass. Jack lit himself a cigarette. He hadn't smoked in years but always kept a packet in the house, for days like these. Jack was grateful for the feeling he got from inhaling the nicotine. He downed the whiskey in one then poured himself another. Then he opened the laptop and switched on the live feed.

Jane was sitting on her sofa reading a book. He couldn't see Les in the house at all. Jack noticed she was wearing a fluffy onesie and had reading glasses on. She looked so content, so comfy and relaxed. Then he heard the door slam and saw Jane throw her glasses on the chair, curl up in ball, and pretended to be asleep. Les walked in and banged about in the kitchen, slamming cupboards and drawers. He was clearly intoxicated with alcohol or drugs. Jack couldn't work out which. He sat there with his eyes transfixed on the screen. His brow began to sweat, and his sister's face kept flitting in and out of his head. Jack cursed himself to fix up and concentrate. Les walked in to the front room and went over to where Jane was pretending to sleep.

Jack noticed the look in Les' eyes, and suddenly he felt the hatred filling his body. He felt the anger rise. Jack wanted to get in his car and go straight over there. He knew he couldn't. Jack needed to plan his every move. There was no way this contract was fucking up, because Jack couldn't hold his own emotions together. What the fuck was this about? Jack was a gangster; he was bigger than feeling down in the fucking dumps. He didn't let shit get to him and was the king of not giving a fuck. Jack told himself "Pull yourself together and concentrate on the job in hand." He took another whiskey and got back to focusing on the laptop. Les was still there in the same spot, standing over Jane. Jack wondered what was going through his head.

Then he saw Les pull out his penis and piss all over Jane. Les was laughing as he done it, and the thing that shocked Jack the most was that Jane didn't flinch. This wanker was literally pissing all over her, and she was clearly that used to it that she had trained herself to be still. He pulled up his trousers and went off to bed. After a few minutes Jane sat up and held her head in her hands and sobbed.

Jack couldn't watch her cry. He wanted to take her in his arms and tell her she was going to be OK. He wanted to let her know that in a couple of days, that wanker she calls her husband won't ever be able to violate her again. Jack wanted to protect her the same way he protected his sister. The next morning, Jack woke up on the sofa. He had finally fallen asleep after a few more whiskeys. Jack was still fully clothed and his mouth tasted like a cesspit.

He yawned and rubbed his head suddenly, realising that drinking that much whiskey wasn't such a great idea. Jack had loads to do that day, so needed to get his arse in to gear. After a quick shower, shit, and shave, Jack was ready to get to work. He turned on the laptop to check up on Jane and to see what his next victim was up to.

Jack was pleased to see that Jane was up and drinking a cup of something hot in her kitchen. Jane looked deep in thought, but she certainly looked better than she did last night. Les came down stairs, picked up his keys from the kitchen side, and walked straight out of the front door. They didn't even acknowledge each other. Jane just sat there staring into space. Jack wondered what she was thinking in that pretty little head of hers. She looked like she had the weight of the world on her shoulders. Jack knew that Les was a car salesman, and he decided to go and take a look in his garage. He pulled up in his Mercedes and watched Les, as he showed this blonde woman around a Corsa. Damn, he thought he was the dog's bollocks.

He was laughing with her and flirting with her; he would do anything to make a sale. Les looked over at Jack and saw his lush Mercedes. It wasn't often cars like that pulled up on his forecourt, and he suddenly thought that money was to be made with this classy bloke. He called one of his junior salesmen over and asked them to take care of the blonde, while he dealt with the new customer.

Jack got out of his car and locked it. The whole time he kept his eyes on Les. He knew he was making him nervous, and he loved that. "Hello sir. Can I help you?" Jack decided to pause before answering just for effect. "I hope so. I'm looking for a little run around for the Mrs, you know nothing to flash. I don't want her turning heads or anything."

Les laughed and said, "Absolutely we can't have that. Can we? And I bet you don't want her driving that car of yours. What a beauty that is." "Yeah, that's right. You know women drivers ain't the best. Plus I don't really want people associating the wife with me in certain circles that I move in, if you know what I mean." "I know exactly what you mean. Keep the wife sweet back at home, but once you shut the front door on your way out, it's time to remove the ball and chain. I totally get it."

"I had a feeling you would." Les thought that comment was a bit odd but shrugged it off, as he could see this man had money. And other than sex that was what excited Les the most. "Take a look at this lovely little fiesta that has just come in, 80,000 on the clock, 1.1 engine, five doors, and immaculate condition in and out." Jack watched him walk around the car giving it the big salesman patter, and all Jack could think about was how much he wanted this guy to suffer. He wanted him to suffer the way that he saw Jane suffer.

This kill had to be slightly different. It had to be special. This punk needed to feel pain. Les interrupted his thoughts by opening the car door and asking Jack to get in, which he did. "Yeah, looks ideal. I am pretty sure she would like it." Jack looked around the shit heap of a car that this little dickhead was trying to sell him. It was shit, and Jack would never buy it, even if he really did need a car.

Les asked him, "So what do you think, fancy a test drive?" "You know what? That would be really great, but I have got to get to a meeting. What time do you close today?" "Around about 8." "Any chance I could come back at closing for a quick test drive? Then I will settle up with you in cash, if that is ok with you?" "Fine by me mate. We close at 8, but I will stick around until 9, as I have some paperwork to sort out anyway. So just pop back later." "Great, thanks. I will see you later." With that Jack shook his hand and looked deep in to his eyes. Les said, "I will look forward to it." Jack sniggered to himself thinking how much he was looking forward to it, too but for so many different reasons.

It was nearer 9 p.m. when Jack turned up at the garage. He got a cab to drop him off a few streets away and walked the rest. Les had nearly given up hope and was just about to call it a day, when he saw Jack walk in. "Sorry I am late. Any chance of that test drive?" "Bloody hell, I was just about to lock up. Thought you had changed your mind." "No. I was waiting on a cab to bring me here, so I can drive the car back after." "Oh right. Yeah. Good idea. You wouldn't want to leave your Merc on my forecourt. I would have to give it a spin." Les laughed but Jack remained silent. "Right, so I will just go and get the car keys and lock up this place. I won't be a minute."

Jack walked out and stood by the red Fiesta. He was looking forward to this. Les came out shortly afterwards and chucked the keys at Jack. "Let's get this show on the road then hey." They both got in the car, and Jack switched on the engine and put it in to first. Les started his sales patter, and Jack told him not to bother. "Listen mate. No need to sell it to me. Consider it sold." "Lovely jubbley, so shall we make our way back to the garage to sort the paperwork?" "If you don't mind, I'm going to stop off at mine to get the cash. I didn't trust myself with all that cash walking the streets." "Oh right, well it's getting late. How about you drop me at the garage and settle up tomorrow?" "Don't be silly. How do you know I will come back?" "Well I don't think you're that silly as to steal the car. I mean I have got family in law enforcement" Jack laughed. "Are you threatening me?" Les laughed. " No, Of course not. It's just I have got a lot on tonight, need to make it back." "Stop worrying. I will take you back, as soon as I give you the cash." Les knew there was no point in arguing with this man. Plus on the upside if he picked up the cash, he could go to his favourite strip bar and get fucked literally. Suddenly Les didn't seem to mind this little road trip.

They pulled up at this small farmhouse in the middle of nowhere. Les was amazed at how much spare land surrounded the house. It had a massive driveway, which Les estimated was as big as his forecourt. "Wow mate! This place is massive. Have you lived here long?" "No." "I can't believe how much spare land you have got. Bloody hell, you could build a housing estate on that and be quid's in." "Suppose I could but not really my thing." "So what do you do?" "Fucking hell, what are you, CID?" Les laughed. "Sorry, I can be a bit of a nosey git, always have been, just my nature." Jack stopped the car and said, "You might as well come in, so we can sort this cash." Les was hoping he would get to have a look inside. They both got out of the car and walked up the driveway. Jack opened the front door and gestured Les to go ahead.

Jack turned on the light, and the first thing Les noticed was the house was completely bare except for a large table. "Shit, you really have only just

LAYLA LOWE

moved in. You ain't even got no furniture." Les turned around to look at Jack, only to notice that Jack was now wearing a clown mask. "What the fuck? What you doing? Are you trying to freak me out? Do you think this shit is funny?" Jack remained silent and still. Les suddenly felt nervous. This guy was a fucking freak. He needed to get out of there and quick. "Listen mate, I don't know what you're playing at, but I ain't got time for games. I have to go." He moved towards the front door, and Jack stood in front of it, so he couldn't get out. "What is your fucking problem, you fucking weirdo? I told you already; I got family in the police force. They ain't going to have this. You are making a huge mistake. You really don't want to fuck with me." Jack moved closer and got right up into Les's face. "Are you scared?" "Are you taking the piss?"

He pushed Jack out of his face, and Jack laughed hysterically. Les didn't know what to do with himself, so he shrugged past Jack and tried to open the door. He pulled on the handle, but the door wouldn't budge. Jack continued to laugh. "What's up Les? The party is just getting started, and you already want to leave. Now why don't you just take a seat? Oh I forgot? There isn't any seats." Jack laughed again. Les was getting really pissed off now. This shit wasn't funny, and whoever set him up is really going to regret it. "Look you sick fuck, open the fucking door!" "Or what? Hey, what are you going to do?" Les decided he needed to knock this cocky little fucker out. He ran at Jack and jumped on top of him. However Jack just caught him and slammed him hard on the floor.

Jack started kicking him in the head, the stomach, and groin area, just like he saw Les do to Jane. Les was rolling on the floor, holding his genitals in pain. Jack kicked him in the head and shouted, "How does it feel cunt!" Les was spitting blood, and his busted nose was bleeding all over his face. "What's your problem? What do you want from me?" "I don't want shit from you! Don't you see all I want is to see you in pain? I don't like you. I know your family, you fucking idiot. I know all about you and how you treat that pretty little wife of yours." "What is this about, that silly fucking retard Jane? Are you serious?" "Shut the fuck up!" Jack grabbed his baseball bat and whacked Les over the head. Les fell unconscious, which gave Jack the chance to set up his tools.

When Les finally came around, everything was a blur. He tried to open his eyes, but only one eye would open. His head was pounding, and then he started to remember the situation he was in. He tried to stand up only to find that he was chained to the table. He looked around as best he could, with his only working eye. The place was quiet. He couldn't see the freak that brought him here, but he could feel he wasn't alone. Les heard a strange noise and could see a small, flashing red light, in the top corner of the room. He suddenly realised that he was being filmed. What the fuck is going on? This shit can't be happening. Seriously, this kind of stuff didn't happen to Les. He was a man to be reckoned with; he was a man to be fearful of.

Clearly this lunatic didn't know who he was dealing with. He told himself to think. "Come on Les. Stay calm. Think of a way to get out of this." Jack entered the room. "Finally decided to join me did you?" Jack was still wearing the clown mask, which he thought was a great addition to this evening's shenanigans. Jack showed Les his axe. "I sharpened this just for you." Jack raised the axe above his head, and Les screamed, "Noooooooooooooo!" "Whack!"

One clean swipe and his hand fell to the floor. His arm was bleeding profusely. Literally blood was squirting everywhere, and Jack just laughed, which he thought added to the hysteria of the situation. Les passed out. When Les finally regained consciousness, his arm was in a bandage, and he was lying on concrete. Now what was going on? He realised that he was outside and thought this was his chance to make a run for it. Les managed to pull himself up slightly, only to find that the chains attached to his arms and neck only allowed him to move so far.

He couldn't believe this shit was happening and started to shout, "Help! Someone please help me!" Jack popped his masked face around the back of the car and said, "There ain't no point in shouting. No one will hear you. Now let's go on a little drive, cause I know how much you like this car." Jack got into the driver's seat and held his rosary beads tight. He said a silent prayer as usual and then slammed the car door; he started to rev the engine. It took a couple of minutes for Les to realise he was actually chained to the car. "No. Please, please don't do this." Jack put his foot down, and the car sped away, dragging Les along with it. He felt the skin on his back getting scraped off. The pain was horrendous. He was screaming in agony, and Jack just drove faster. His head and body bounced over the concrete surface of the car park and over the field. Les lost consciousness at some point. He also lost his arm, and most of his face was scrapped to shreds along the way. The skin on his whole body was being literally shredded.

Jack drove to the lake, which was just beyond the fields surrounding the little farmhouse. It wasn't until the night before that Jack thought about bringing him there. Jack bought this place years ago, obviously with cash. He had planned to live in it, but he never did. Jack got out of the car and picked up what was left of Les. He shoved him into the boot of the car, took off the handbrake, and pushed the car in to the lake. As Jack watched the car slowly sink, he stood there in silence. Jack was pleased with himself. He was pleased that Jane no longer had to worry about this wanker abusing her; he was pleased at the additions he had made to his little killing routine, like the mask and the axe.

Jack was so good at this shit. He even shocked himself. Jack walked back to the house and got showered and changed. He put his clothes into the open fire and let them burn. It was really late now, and he was so tired. Jack was going to go home but thought he may as well spend the night, as the upstairs of the house was fully kitted out. He could go to church in the morning before going home. Jack got into bed, and as soon as his head hit the pillow, he was out like a light.

CHAPTER 6

THE LAST CONFESSION:

THIS IS PERSONAL

Father Patrick slammed the door of the confession booth and stomped to his office. He had around £30.000 in his hand, and he didn't want it. The bishop was on the phone in the office. And when he saw Father Patrick storm in to the room, he decided to say a quick goodbye and hang up. Father Patrick chucked the money on the table in front of the bishop. "There you go. There is your blood money. Take it. Have it all, because I don't want any part of it. I have just sat and listened to a man tell me how he beat a guy to death. How he dragged his body around a car park using a car; how he enjoyed seeing him in pain; and how proud of his work he is. I can't do this anymore. This is not what I signed up for. This shit just isn't right!"

"Calm down Patrick."

The bishop poured them both a brandy, and Patrick knocked his back in one huge gulp. "You say I have to listen to this man and offer him support. But tell me Bishop. How can I support the devil? How can I accept money from Satan himself? There is not one shred of kindness in that man. I would go as far as to say he isn't human; he must be demonic."

"Calm down Patrick. Please just take a breath and try to relax. You know as well as I do that God sends us tests to see our faith pushed, to the absolute limit. This is your test Patrick. This is God's way of testing your faith and your loyalty to him. Those vows you took were taken under God. Now your test has come, and you want out just like that." "I never said I want out. I love my job. And for the most part I enjoy what I do, but this is too much. I preach to stop fighting and war. I preach love, unity and peace. This man is the total opposite to everything I believe in." "Yes, he is, and God has sent him to you. Be there for the man, and maybe in time he will change. Everything happens for a reason, and that reason isn't always clear Patrick. Stay strong and continue your good work, and God will in time reward you." With that the Bishop picked up the cash, put it in his bag, and walked out of the room.

Father Patrick sank in his chair and poured himself another brandy. "Please God help me. Set me free from evil." Father Patrick laid his head in his hands and cried for the first time in years. Jack walked out of the church with a huge smile on his face. That was his best confession yet. He told the story so well. Jack could have made a movie out of it. That thought made him laugh, as he remembered in around about way that he already did make a movie of it. He laughed out loud, as he got in to his car. Jack was just about to start up the engine, when he heard his phone ring. "Hello?" "Jack is that you?" "Yes. Hey Amy. How are you?" The call went silent for what seemed like ages. "Ames, you still there?" "Jack I need you to meet me at the hospital. I am in Accident and Emergency." "What's happened?" The line went dead, and jack instantly chucked his phone on the seat and sped off, making his way to the hospital.

Every scenario played over in his head. Was it the boys? Had they had an accident? Was it Amy? Was she hurt? What the fuck? The unknown was making him crazy. He was bibbing his horn for people to move out of his way, only to be bibbed back at in return. The traffic was chocka block, and to top it off he had some dumb arse, fucking learner driver in front of him. He decided to overtake and shout abuse at the young lad driver, as he went past. The learner driver was so scared that he stalled the car and caused another driver to crash in to the back of him. Jack didn't care. He needed to get to Amy fast, and as far as he was concerned, the whole world needed to get out of his fucking way.

LAYLA LOWE

When Jack finally reached the hospital, he was physically shaking. He walked in to the emergency room, ignoring the staff who asked him to wait. He saw Amy's husband, no kids, no Amy, just her husband. "Where is she?" "Jack you need to calm down." "Don't tell me to calm down, you pathetic little prick! Where is my sister, and where are my boys!" Jack grabbed the terrified man by his neck and shoved him against the wall. "Tell me!" Steve tried to talk but couldn't actually breath. The doctor came rushing over and got in between them. He shouted for Jack to calm down. "Where is my sister?" "Amy is in room 5, and the boys are at their mate's house. For fuck sake Jack, you didn't give me a chance." Jack was already opening the door to room 5, before Steve had finished his sentence. Steve let him go. He knew when he wasn't wanted. Amy jumped with fright and looked up from her bed straight at her brother. A deep silence drowned the room. Jack couldn't speak. He couldn't even move; he was simply frozen to the ground by shock. Amy started to sob, which snapped Jack back to reality. He went over to her and held her in his arms.

Amy's face was swollen. Her eyes were only slits and were black and puffy. She had a fat lip and a missing front tooth. Her hair was tangled, and Jack thought she looked like she had been attacked. He pulled himself away from her, looked into her face and asked, "Amy love, who done this to you?" Amy tried to stop crying and finally managed to tell her brother what had happened, on what started out to be a normal day. "It was just like any other day Jack. I woke up, got the boy's breakfast, and argued with Nat about what clothes he could wear to his mates birthday party. Just the usual really. I took the boys to the party and decided to leave them both there, whilst I done some shopping. It is so much harder doing the food shop with the boys you know. I wanted for once to do it in peace." Jack nodded. "Go on."

Amy took a deep breath and squeezed her brothers hand, as she recalled what happened to her next. "I went to Sainsbury's, done the shopping, and was loading it in the car boot, when I felt someone grab me." She paused and wiped away tears. Jack took a deep breath, as he felt like he was going to explode but knew he had to keep it together. "Go on Amy. What happened next?"

"I quickly tried to turn around, but he had me so tight that I couldn't. He had his hand over my mouth, so I couldn't even scream." "He told me to do as I was told, or he would kill me. I froze. He picked me up and threw me on the concrete, in front of my car. I looked around to see if I could signal for help, but no one was about. I felt his hand go up my dress, and I tried to break free. He punched me in the face and whacked my head on the floor. He seemed angry Jack, like I had done something wrong to him. I remember looking up at him, and his face was like stone. He ripped my tights and…"

Amy couldn't speak any more. The tears had got the better of her. She wiped her face with a tissue and watched her brothers face drain of color, as what she told him sank in. "Go on Amy. I need to know everything." "He ripped my tights and raped me." Tears fell down Jack's face, as he had flash backs of his dad raping Amy as a child. This beautiful girl had been through so much. "When he finished, he got up as I lay there, too afraid to move. He told me that he knew I liked it. That he knew that I was a slag, when he saw me. Then he kicked me in my stomach, and he must of hit me in the head again, as I lost consciousness. The next thing I knew I was here." Amy sobbed, and Jack held her close, just like he did all those years ago. "I am so sorry Amy. I'm so sorry that I wasn't there to protect you. I should have been there." He was crying into her long blonde hair.

All Amy could do was sob and hold her brother tight. After a few minutes Jack broke away, pulled up a chair, and took his sisters hand. "Amy I need you to think really hard. I know this is really hard for you, but I need you to tell me what he looked like." "I don't want to remember Jack. I never want to see his face again." "I know that sweetheart, but I promise you that after you do this, you will never have to speak of him again." Amy took a deep breath and closed her eyes. "He was tall; he had brown long hair tied in a ponytail; he had his hood up, but it fell off. And I noticed his long hair. He had hard dark brown eyes and yellow crooked teeth."

"Good girl. Anything else can you remember, anything else like what he was wearing?" "He had a black tracksuit on with a hood. I remember his trainers were white but dirty. I remember looking at his trainers as he kicked me, and he had bad skin. Yes. That is right. He had bad skin and bad teeth. He was young though Jack, must of only have been in his twenties."

Jack was digesting all of the information that Amy was giving him. All he kept thinking about was how scared Amy must have been. What kind of scum bag done that sort of thing, especially in pure day light? It had taken his sister years to be able to trust a man properly, after their dad broke her. But she was happy now with her husband and her boys. She didn't deserve this. Jack thought back to his confession. Was this Karma? Was this his fault? Anyone who knows him knows that he doesn't give a fuck about anything. He will deal with whatever is thrown at him, but when it comes down to his sister and her boys, he wasn't fucking about. Jack would literally kill for them. Amy watched her brother as he sat in silence, and she knew he was blaming himself for not being able to prevent this. She loved her brother with all of her heart, and she never blamed him. Amy blamed herself. Maybe her dress was too short, or she was sending out the wrong messages. Her dad raped her, and now she had been brutalized by a passing stranger.

What was it about her that screamed out victim? Why did these men think it was OK to abuse her body, mess with her head, and treat her like she was no better than the shit on their shoe? What the fuck? Unbeknown to Amy, she was actually crying and Jack watched her, as she tortured herself over what happened. "Amy, I'm going to sort this."

"How can you possibly sort this Jack! It has happened. I see him when I close my eyes. I feel him. I smell him. There is nothing anyone can do to take that away from me Jack. I know this, because I still wake up in a cold sweat after having a nightmare about dad. I can still smell him Jack. I can smell the alcohol on his breath. I can feel his sweat drip on my face. It never goes away Jack, never. I am married. I have kids. I live in a nice house and have coffee mornings with the school mums. On the outside I look normal, but on the inside I know I am dirty. I am used and abused. I am trash. I am ruined, and all this has done is prove to me that you can't make a whore into a house wife Jack"

She was really sobbing now, and Jack was shocked to hear her talk about herself like that. "Amy, you are a beautiful woman, a great mum, wife, and the best sister I could ever have asked for. You mean the world to me and your little family. This isn't a reflection on you Ames. This is just the fucked up society that we live in. Amy please don't think that of yourself, please" He hugged her and squeezed her tight. "I love you sis."

Amy sobbed on her brother's shoulder. Jack held her until she fell asleep. It was dark when jack finally left his sisters side. He made sure that her husband was staying the night with her. Jack rang Amy's friend and neighbor who agreed to take care of the boys. He wanted to see the boys, but knew he needed to see Paul more. Jack phoned Paul but got no answer. That just irritated Jack more. He was normally so careful about keeping his distance from Paul, due to their working relationship, but tonight wasn't about Paul and his career. Tonight was about Jack's sister, and Paul will just have to deal with it.

He walked into the police station and waited patiently in the que. There was a drunk male in front of him, shouting the odds at the desk Sargent. Jack was patient for at least two minutes, but he couldn't take much more of this piss taking tramp. So he simply pushed him out of the way and stood at the desk, in front of the Sargent. The drunk was absolutely enraged that he had been pushed out of the way. Who the fuck did this dude think he was? "Hey mate, watch who you are fucking pushing. I was here first." Jack ignored him. "Hi, can you call Chief Inspector Paul Burrows down for me please?" "Is he expecting you?" "No, but he will see me. So if you could just call him, I would be most grateful." The Sargent thought about it for a second. "What is it regarding?" "Its personal. Can you just tell him Jack is here?"

The Sargent picked up the phone. As he was speaking, he looked at Jack. He didn't expect the chief to say he would see him and was shocked, when he asked him to bring Jack to his office. He put the phone down and told Jack to follow him. The drunk saw red and couldn't believe this ponce was being seen before him. "Oi, your taking the fucking piss mate. I was here first. What about me?" Both Jack and the officer ignored him and continued to the chief's office in silence.

Paul was waiting at his office door. He had a face like thunder, but Jack didn't give a fuck. He ushered Jack into his office and shut the door behind him. Jack sat down. "What the fuck are you doing here? Are you out of your fucking mind? Are you trying to fuck me up or what?" Jack let Paul have his rant, and after about three minutes he had had enough. "Alright Paul firstly, shut the fuck up. For once this ain't about you for fuck sake. Secondly, talk to me like that again, and your arse is mine do you understand? Thirdly, from tonight you work for me, and I ain't fucking playing?" "Are you taking the fucking piss Jack? Are you actually trying to threaten me?"

"I don't threaten people Paul. You should know that. I deal with what needs to be done. I have done several jobs for you, one of which is on this disk." Jack chucked the recording from yesterday at Paul. "Now you came to me, when you had a family problem that needed to be sorted. What did I do Paul? I will tell you what; I fucking dealt with it. I made your problem disappear. Now I have a family problem, and you are going to deal with it for me." Paul was totally gob smacked. He couldn't believe what was going on. This contract killer, his contract killer was in his office calling the shots. Was this a fucking dream or what? "It's Amy. She has been attacked." "What do you mean attacked?"

"I mean she has had a trip to the fucking hairdressers. What the fuck do you think I fucking mean? Some cunt has attacked her, raped her, beat her black and fucking blue. That is what I am talking about." Paul took the whiskey he kept in his top drawer out and poured both of them a shot. Jack was grateful for the burn, as he felt the alcohol hit the back of his throat. Both men sat in silence for a while. Paul was going over what Jack had said in his head. He knew Jack better to know that he wouldn't be here for something trivial.

Paul also knew how much Amy meant to Jack. He would help as best he could, but he wasn't going to lose his career over this shit. "So how is Amy?" "I think she is finally broken, beyond fixing. She is black and blue and hurting all over, but it's the emotional scars I'm worried about. You should have heard her today. She told me how much she hated herself; how she was disgusting and trash. I can't have that Paul. She is the best woman I know. She is kind to a fault, and her only crime in her whole life is to have been too trusting." Paul listened and agreed with Jack.

Paul had actually met Amy before, not that she would remember, as she was only young. But he could tell she was a sweet kid, and he followed both her and Jack's life closely from then on. He knew Jack was going to grow into a bad ass. And for some reason he took pity on them, after being called to the flat they lived in with their parents, one night when he was a PC. Paul had never witnessed such neglect, and from that moment he decided to look out for them.

It became obvious to Paul early on that Jack was a born killer, so he decided to use that to his advantage. The rest is history. Jack took the whiskey bottle and poured another shot. "Are the police involved?" "Yeah. Apparently they took a statement from Amy before I got to the hospital. The lady that found her called them and an ambulance by all accounts. Personally I wouldn't of bothered calling your lot, as I would have preferred to deal with it myself. But truth is I don't know where to start looking. When I get my jobs, I know where they are, and I know what they have done. This time all I have is Amy's description, and that is why I am here."

"Well Jack, rest assured I will make this case a priority of mine. I will talk to the team in charge, and when I am in the know, so will you be. You have my word." "Thanks Paul. That is good enough for me." Jack got up to leave, and Paul followed him to the door. "Listen Jack, I am sorry that this has happened to Amy, but promise me you will leave it with me, until I have firm evidence against the perpetrator. Don't do anything silly." Jack looked at Paul and said, "I look forward to hearing from you, very soon." Paul knew that was an underlying threat, but he couldn't blame him.

Jack walked into to his cold house. He switched the light on and headed straight for the whiskey. Jack didn't even get a glass. He drank it straight from the bottle; he needed it; he needed to get so drunk that he would just sleep, like he was in a coma. Jack was so tired, but his mind just would not stop turning over all of the information Amy had given him. Long brown hair, bad skin, bad teeth and young, the thoughts just kept coming.

What the fuck was it with the younger generation these days? They have no fucking respect. That was the problem. They are raised in a time when it is a crime to punish your kids. They get whatever they want and spend most of their adolescent life killing people on the computer. It's no wonder when they finally hit the street, they take what they want no matter how they have to get it. Well this little fucker was going to wish he never entered the car park that day. That he never spotted Amy loading her shopping. That he had never had that ugly urge to beat, rape, and degrade her, like she was worth shit. He would regret fucking with Jack's family. That little cunt was going to hurt and hurt bad, until he died. And Jack was going to enjoy every minute of it. This shit was personal! Jack finished the bottle and made his way to his bed. He knew he would sleep now, as he could hardly keep his eyes open. His last thought before he closed his eyes and gave into sleep was of Amy, his beautiful sister lying in that hospital bed, hurting and hating herself.

Paul walked into work the next day on a mission. The quicker he finds out who attacked Amy the better. He needed Jack in his right frame of mind. Crazy Jack was frightening, but beyond crazy Jack was not worth thinking about. Detective Dan walked into the chief's office and instantly felt nervous. "Sir, you wanted me." "That is right. Sit down and tell me what you have on the rape case, of the lady in the car park." Dan wasn't expecting that question. He thought he was in for a telling off; he thought someone had clicked that most of the time he spends on duty he is actually pissed as a newt.

"Well actually sir, we are linking this case to at least four others. All of which happened to single ladies, who were alone and either having car trouble or like the most recent lady, loading her car with shopping. All cases took place in car parks; all of the victims were beaten and raped. And they all described a white, young male in his twenties with long brown hair. That is all we have at the moment sir." "And any suspects?" "A couple of leads, but I am not sure what will come of those yet." "When are you following up on those leads?" "Well I have a couple of other cases so probably on Wednesday." "Wrong answer."

Dan looked at the chief and didn't know what to say to that. "This is now your only case. I suggest you pass your other cases to a colleague. Pick another colleague to work with you on this case, and this case gets all of your attention. Do you understand?" "Yes sir." "Right, I want a report at the end of every working day, and if I am not around, you can call my mobile. If you don't keep me informed and I have to come looking for you, I suggest you get a copy of the local newspaper and start looking for another job." "Yes sir." "Oh and Dan, I will be watching you very closely on this case. If you fuck up, say goodbye to your career and your policeman pension. If you get me the result I need quickly, consider your self promoted." "Promoted sir, you mean detective inspector?"

"No Dan. Don't be ridiculous. I would never be stupid enough to promote a fucking drunk would I? But I give you my word that you will keep your current position and pension, if you deliver. And trust me Dan. That should be fucking music to your ears, because I really want you out. Now go and do what I fucking pay you for." Dan walked out of the office quickly. He knew there was no point arguing with the chief. Dan knew he had just been given a lifeline, and he was going to take it.

Nat was surprised to see his Uncle Jack knock on his neighbour's door. "Hey Uncle Jack. How did you know I was here?" "Hey Natty boy. I told you already. I know everything." Nat laughed as Jack picked him up and playfully chucked him in the air.

It took Nat a couple of minutes to recover, when Jack finally put him down. "Have you seen my mummy Jack, because Sheila said she is in the hospital, and I am worried about her." "Don't you go worrying about your mum Nat. She is in good hands and will be home soon, making you tidy your room and eat your veg. She just had a little accident, nothing to worry about."

The thought of eating veg and cleaning his room made Nat feel grateful for being next door. He ran off to play without a second thought. Jack spent some time with baby Jackson and had a cup of tea with Sheila. He knew that she knew the truth, but he also knew she wasn't stupid enough to try and talk to Jack about it. His phone rang, and he instantly jumped up to answer it. "Hello it's me." "Yeah, what you got for me." "Nothing yet, but my guys are following up some leads today." "Following up some leads? Don't give me that bullshit. I don't want to talk to you, until you get me some names. I want to know the names of the leads they are following up, cause I will follow them up too."

"OK Jack. Stay calm. I will get you what you need." "Make sure you do, because the longer I am left waiting the more time I have to think. And the more time I spend thinking means I have more time to plan my next move. As you know when I have a thirst on, I can't hang around. So if you don't give me those suspects, I might have to come to your fucking station and let your people know how fucking pissed off I am." "OK Jack. I get the message. As I said, I will get you those names." Jack hung up, gave Sheila back her cup, kissed the boys, and went home to prepare. He knew he would have those names before the day was up, because Paul knows not to play with him.

Amy was worried. She hadn't seen her brother all day, and she knew how badly he had taken her attack. He takes everything so personal. She knows that he can't help it. It is just his way. Amy was worried not just about how he was feeling, but what he would do next.

Paul was in his office drinking whiskey and shouting down the phone to Dan. "I want to know who you are checking out Dan! I told you already when you know something, I want to fucking know. Is that really so fucking hard to understand?" "OK Chief. I hear you. I am on my way back to the station. I will meet you in your office with everything I have got." Dan was fuming. Who the fuck did the chief think he was? Half the time he didn't even acknowledge him in the corridor, and now he is on his back 24 fucking 7.The sooner this case was over the better. Dan walked into Paul's office without even knocking. He was not in the mood for Paul's high-ranking fucking attitude.

If he lost his job, so fucking be it. It was late, and he was tired from chasing around after the fucking chief all day. Dan placed the folders on the table and sat down. "So we have narrowed it down to two suspects. Both have previous sex offences, mainly minor stuff, flashing in public, stealing underwear, stalking ex- girlfriends, and shit like that. However one of them has got a broken leg and has had it for three weeks now. So that rules him out." Dan reached for a folder. "That leaves us with this sad little fuck." He took out photographs of a white male.

"His name is Lee Watson. He lives at home with his grandmother on the kings estate. He has been in and out of care as a child. Mother was a prostitute working the streets from about 14. Fuck knows who his dad is, and what can I say. He was born a wrongen. He is a hard little fucker who can definitely hold his own with the best of them. All case reports since he was 8 years old have said that he has an unhealthy interest in the opposite sex, and he was even accused of attempted rape at the age 15." "OK. I get it. He is a sick fuck, but what makes him number one suspect?"

"Well this is where I had to put my detective hat on, and to be honest it wasn't hard to link him. The CCTV from the Sainsbury car park catches him entering and leaving on the same day, and guess what? Around the same time of the attack on the last victim. To be honest I haven't had time to look at CCTV from the other cases, but I would bet my pension on it being him." "OK. That's good work Dan. Now I want you to leave this with me." "What? What do you mean leave it with you? I have already planned kicking his door down at 6 a.m. His arse is mine!"

"Correction Dan, your arse is mine. You got that? So I say for you, this job is done. Now go home, sleep off the alcohol, and see you bright and early, ready for work in the morning." "What?" "You heard me Dan. Fuck off before I change my mind." Dan stood up and stomped out of the office, slamming the door behind him. He was fuming. That work was his, and now that jumped up shit head was going to take all of the fucking credit.

Paul phoned Jack as soon as Dan left. "Hello?" "Hello it's me." "No shit; now what you got for me?" "Lee Watson lives on the Kings estate. I have emailed you a photo. Pretty sure this is your man." "Great. Leave it with me from now on." "Don't worry. I have already called off the dogs, but make sure he aint found will you? As that will just be too much explaining for me to do." Paul put the phone down without waiting for a response. He knew Jack was a professional; he knew that he wouldn't fuck up, but he also knew this was the last time Jack fucking gave the orders."

Jack stared at the mug shot that Paul had sent him. It was clear to Jack why this little fucker had to rape girls. He was one ugly shit! Anyone waking up next to him in the dark would surly think they were having a nightmare. Jack grabbed his already prepared bag and headed to the Kings estate. He sat outside of the flat for hours, until he saw Lee come out. He watched as he lit up a cigarette and then pulled his hood up over his head.

Lee strutted down the street, like he was God's fucking gift. Jack remained seated for a couple of minutes, not taking his eye off him. He held his rosary beads, muttered a quick prayer, took a swig of his whiskey, and got out of the car. Jack had his bag over one shoulder and a woolen beanie hat on his head. He was dressed all in black and was wearing steel cap boots, like he had just got off a shift on a building site or something.

Then Jack followed Lee, as he walked into the park entrance. Lee was still on his own, but his strut had turned into a slow shifty walk now. And Jack wondered what had changed his demeanor all of a sudden. Jack then spotted the two girls coming towards them. Both were in heels; both walking like they were under the influence and giggling their heads off. Lee went and stood behind a tree.

Jack couldn't believe his eyes. Was this wanker going to attack these girls? Surely he wasn't. There were two of them for fuck sake. That was risky, even for the most professional fucking pervert. Jack stood behind another tree a little way back from Lee. He was sure he wasn't spotted, as Lee was now transfixed on these two young girls. The girls had absolutely no clue about the fact that they were being watched. They continued walking down the path, linking arms and laughing overly loud about fuck all. When they reached the park entrance, the girls stood for a couple of minutes chatting. Jack couldn't believe it when they hugged and started to say goodbye.

Are these girls for real? Are they really going to split up and leave each other in the fucking dark park? No way! Jack looked over at Lee and saw that he was already putting his gloves on. This cunt was going to pounce. One of the girls started walking back through the park, in her high heels and short skirt. She wasn't even concentrating, as she was too busy texting on her phone. Jack felt like grabbing her and giving her a slap himself, for being so fucking stupid.

She continued to walk and must of heard something, as she looked back. She seemed to look straight at Jack, but obviously she couldn't have seen him, as she carried on walking deeper in to the darkness of the park. Jack wanted to shout and tell her to run, but he knew he had to just shut up and follow him following her. The girl was obviously a little spooked, as she quickened up a bit. But those stupid fucking shoes weren't helping.

Suddenly Lee was right behind her. He grabbed her and dragged her into the trees. She was trying to fight and obviously couldn't scream, cause he had his hand over her mouth. Jack went into the clearing of the trees, where Lee had chucked her on the floor. Jack heard him say, "I knew you was a little slut, as soon as I saw you"

Amy flashed in to Jack's mind, and he froze for a few seconds. This was definitely his man; this was definitely the guy that attacked his Amy. With that thought in his head, he opened his bag and pulled out a crowbar. The girl was on the ground begging for Lee to let her go. She was crying and visibly shaking. Jack came up behind Lee and whacked him over the back of his head, with his crowbar. Lee instantly fell to the ground, right next to his intended victim. She was screaming. Jack grabbed her and shouted, "Shut up for fuck sake will you! I am not going to hurt you."

The girl continued to whimper, and her breathing was heavy and rapid. "Now listen to me, take this money, go left out of the park, and get a taxi home. There is a cab office in the next street. Take them fucking shoes off, run, and don't stop running until you are there. But listen. When you get there, you tell nobody nothing, cause I need to sort this sick little fucker out." "Yes, yes, yes, please let me go." "Wait one second. If you tell anyone about me, I will hunt you down." "Yes, I promise." "When you tell the police about this, you don't mention me. Do you understand? I just saved you girl, and you need to be more careful in the future." "I will. Please let me go." "OK. Now run." The girl didn't need to be told twice. She was gone before Jack could even take a breath.

He dragged Lee's body over to the trees, nearest to the entrance. He covered him over with leaves and branches. Lee was still alive, but he wasn't going to be waking up any time soon. Jack left the park and made his way back to the car. He jumped in and drove up to the entrance of the park. There were no street lights, so Jack turned off his car lights too. He opened the car boot and went to collect his prize.

As Jack thought Lee was still out cold, he threw him in the boot and slammed it. He got back into his car and sped off down the road. Jack was pleased with how easily and quickly he had managed to get Lee and get out of there. He drove to the farmhouse in the middle of nowhere. Jack had been there earlier in the day, preparing for this moment. He drove to the middle of the field; he got out of the car and opened the car boot. Jack looked at the pathetic body laying there. He was skinny and looked like he hadn't washed his skin for about 10 years. His hair was shiny with Grease and now blood from his seeping head wound. Jack could pick him up easily, which he did.

He laid him near the wooden pole that he had resurrected earlier. He stripped the boy naked, tied his hands and feet together, before strapping him tightly to the pole. Jack made sure that all of the ropes were tied tight enough, so he couldn't move but not too tight to squeeze the life out of him. That sort of death wasn't good enough for this little fucker. He needed to feel pain. Lee needed to be taught a fucking lesson. This shit was personal to Jack, and he was going to enjoy every minute of it. It was about an hour or so later when Lee began to stir. Jack was in no rush; he was sat in a foldaway camping chair sipping whiskey, thinking what a lovely evening it was. He watched Lee as he tried to move his hands. He lifted his head and opened his eyes. Lee looked at his hands, and the realisation washed over him. He knew he was in shit. Lee instantly felt cold and started to shiver. It hurt when he moved his head, but he knew that he needed to know where he was.

He looked up and saw Jack sitting in a chair, with a drink in his hand like he was fucking camping. "What the fuck is going on? Who are you, and what the fuck do you think you are doing?" Jack didn't say a word. He just stared at the now frightened boy. Jack watched as he wet himself. "What are you going to do to me? Answer me! Answer me!" Jack poured himself another drink and sipped it slowly. "What are you some kind of fucking retard? Cant you talk? Do you think this is funny or something, or are you gay? Is that what this is about? You fancy me, and you are in to some kinky kind of shit. Is that it? Well you need to untie me, cause this aint what I am in to." Jack just stared at him and continued to sip his drink. Lee began to cry.

It was about 20 minutes later when Jack decided to move. He got up and took out a piece of cheese wire that he had looped and knotted. Jack had also added a weight to the end. Lee was just watching, wondering what the fuck this dude was about to do. Jack walked over to him and grabbed his penis. Lee screamed, "What you doing? Help somebody, help!" Jack placed his penis inside the loop and tightened it. He looked into Lee's face and said, "You raped my sister, you ugly little fucker. You beat her, and you raped her. Bet you enjoyed it too. Didn't you? Well let me tell you something. You fucked with the wrong woman! No one fucks with my sister! Do you understand!" "I'm sorry! I'm sorry! Please let me go!" Lee was sobbing now, and Jack looked at him in disgust, as he swung the weighted wire. Lee screamed in agony as the wire tightened and cut into the flesh of his penis. Jack grabbed the weight and held it in his hand. "I'm going to make sure you can't fuck ever again." "No please! Stop! I'm sorry!" Jack swung the weight again, but this time he used more force.

Lee was screaming as the wire sank deeper in to his flesh. The weight fell to the ground along with his penis. Blood was going everywhere and all Jack done was laugh. He went over to his car and pulled out a serving dish lid made of steel along with 3 rats. He put the rats in the lid and pushed the lid onto Lee's stomach. Lee was crying and screaming, as the rats scrambled to get out of the lid, scratching his skin frantically. Jack picked up his blowtorch and began to heat the lid. The rats panicked, scratched, and bit on Lee trying to get out. Lee was screaming and begging Jack to stop, but Jack didn't stop. He continued to hold the lid in place and heat it with his torch. Jack took pleasure in watching, as Lee slipped in and out of consciousness.

The rats literally chewed through Lee's body to escape. Jack took the lid away, and the rats ran off. He looked at the damage they had done and was really quite impressed. This guy was a dirty perverted, sick little rat, and it was only right that he died this way; it was what he deserved. Jack guessed that Lee was dead but decided to leave him straddled to the post, as he profusely bled. Jack had another drink, lit a cigarette, and thought it was a perfect night for a bonfire. Lee seemed to murmur, as Jack poured petrol over Lee's broken body and set it on fire with his blowtorch. It really was quite a show. The flames were high and ferocious; the smell of burning flesh filled the air. Jack sat back in his chair and watched his sister's attacker burn. He couldn't remember the last time he actually felt this satisfied.

CHAPTER 7

GOOD VERSUS EVIL

Jack hadn't slept all night; the same question was rolling around in his head. Was what happened to Amy pay back for the deaths he had caused? Jack had always convinced himself that he worked for the good of mankind. That he was only doing what God needed him to do. It was around midday when Jack finally pulled himself together and walked in to the church. This was a place of comfort, a place of sanctuary, a place he could get the answers he needed. Jack knelt in a pew and prayed. He prayed for his sister; he prayed for his nephews; and he prayed for God to release his soul. Jack wanted to know who he really was. He wanted to know if he was Jack a serial killer, who simply killed because he liked it. Or was he Jack the modern-day Robin Hood?

Father Patrick had seen Jack come in, and his heart simply sank. He couldn't take any more of this shit; he couldn't listen to this man's gruesome explanations of murder and his so-called religious reasons behind it. Father Patrick deserved more respect than this. He walked in to his office, and once again the Bishop was sat in his chair. Since Father Patrick had been bringing in all this money, the Bishop showed up much more often, and Patrick hated all the attention.

"Sorry to disturb you Bishop, but I need you to cover for me this afternoon; I have some errands to run that simply can't wait. I am sure the church will be quiet. Is that OK?" "Of course Patrick. Take the afternoon off. I will simply lock up when I leave." Excellent! Thank you Bishop. I really appreciate it." With that Father Patrick put his coat on and grabbed his bag.

He got to the door and looked back at the Bishop. "Oh by the way, you may want to go to the confession booth. I do believe we have someone waiting. Thanks again cheerio." Father Patrick laughed to himself as he walked out. The relief that he didn't have to listen to a horror story filled him with joy. The Bishop sighed to himself, because he could really do without listening to some drab person tell him some ridiculous confession, about how they had an impure thought or something like that. He found confessions tedious, simply because he knew that the people who confessed never really confessed their true badness. They just told you something minor. No one ever told the real truth.

Jack had been in the church for over an hour.

He was still on his knees praying, when he felt that someone had sat next to him. He opened his eyes to see the Bishop and actually felt nervous. Jack stood up quickly. "Please continue to pray if you feel the need. As I wouldn't want to come between you and God." "No, it's fine. I was just about done anyway." "Do you have something on you mind? As if you don't mind me saying so, you look very drained and tired, like you have the world on your shoulders." "You are right Bishop. I haven't slept all night; I have family troubles. You see, my sister Amy has been attacked, and I can't stop thinking about it. Which in turn has made me question myself about how I lead my life."

"That's understandable son. When something bad happens to someone we love, we will automatically question ourselves about why, how or if we could have done anything to help. Unfortunately we can't control everything that happens around us, and sometimes we feel guilty about that." Jack and the Bishop sat in silence.

The Bishop had realised that this man was the generous donator, and he had also realised why Father Patrick wanted to rush off. However he was glad that he was there. As at some point soon, Father Patrick was going to chicken out of listening to this man's sins. And the money would simply stop coming in. He couldn't have that. "I can see you are upset. Why don't we go in to the office and talk privately?" "Don't you want me to go into the confession box?" "Not really son. I am not too good with confined spaces. If the truth be told, I would rather have a chat in the office, if you don't mind that is." "No. That is fine." Both men stood up, and Jack followed the Bishop down the aisle, which led to the back office.

Jack was impressed; the office was nice and spacious and had all of the latest mod cons, including a coffee machine. The Bishop saw Jack eye up the coffee machine and instantly offered him one. "Would you like a posh coffee? I don't think much of them myself, but Father Patrick swears that posh coffee was sent from Heaven." The Bishop laughed at his own wit, and Jack suddenly felt uneasy. Was this guy for real? The Bishop passed Jack his coffee and pointed to the sugar bowl. "Help yourself to a sugar or two. The sweetness will do you good." Jack scooped two large spoons of sugar and stirred it in to his coffee. Again the men sat in silence.

"So am I correct in thinking that you are Jack?" "Yes. How did you know?" "Father Patrick has told me all about you son." "Really? Like what?" Jack looked at the ground feeling suddenly ashamed of his previous confessions. "Don't worry son. Whatever you tell us remains in the walls of the church. After all you have made a huge difference to our church and the community, with all of your very generous donations. I want you to know how grateful we are." "Thank you Bishop, but to be honest if you knew how I got the money, you probably wouldn't be as grateful." "Not at all son. I know more about you than you think, and as I have told Father Patrick, every man has his demons. Not everyone will think that what you do is the right thing to do Jack, but I think I see things from your point of view." Jack was stunned. Was he really hearing this?

Was this Bishop an undercover cop or something? He sat in silence gathering his thoughts. "I mean what I say Jack. It takes courage to stand up for others, and only a true brave heart would defeat evil and stick up for the innocent. In my book, which I might remind you is the Bible, I find that commending." "Are you serious Bishop, because I feel like you are taking the piss and excuse my language?" "Yes. I am serious. Tell me Jack. Who have you killed and why?" Jack sat for minute or two, wondering if he should tell this Bishop his sins in case it was a set up. He settled the argument with himself by agreeing to talk. Jack truly believed that everything happened for a reason. So if this was some undercover police operation and he was arrested, then that is how God wanted it to go.

"I have had a troubled life Bishop; I have seen things that you wouldn't want your worst enemy to see. Since childhood I have been fighting with evil. My dad was a pedophile, a drunk, a violent despicable man. My mother was a good for nothing druggy whore. My only saving grace was my sister Amy. We are and always have been very close". Jack stopped talking and took a deep breath. "It's

OK. Carry on Jack. I am listening." "Well you see, my sister, she is the nicest person I have ever met. She has always protected me from our parents, and it wasn't until I was about 6 that I realised just what she had to go through, to protect me from them." Jack could feel his emotions rising and told himself to stop being a ponce. He took a sip of the coffee and continued talking.

"You see Bishop, that evil man that was supposed to protect and look after us was using his daughter in the worst possible way. Not only was he beating and bullying her, but he was raping her. I remember walking in Amy's bedroom. My dad was naked, and I remember Amy's face. She looked like she was made of stone. Even then she tried to be strong for me, but that day I saw the world for how it really is. He was our dad; he was supposed to love us, but he degraded us in every way he could.

The beatings got worse, but it was me that started to take the brunt of it. I didn't care, as long as Amy was OK. The beatings became more frequent, but all they done was make me stronger. I refused to let him see me cry. When he beat me, I would imagine killing him. The thought pleased me. It excited me. Is that normal?"

"Well it is a question that doesn't have a simple answer Jack. Your dad was an evil man; he beat you and raped your sister. Who in their right mind wouldn't want to see him dead? Does that make me wrong Jack? Am I wrong, because I would rather see happy children than abused children? Am I wrong, because I would like to see filth like your father punished? I put it to you that I am not wrong Jack. The fact is the world is a mixture of good and evil. All you wanted to do was protect your sibling, which to me is a good thing. It was your dad's actions that put the bad thoughts into your head Jack.

If you didn't experience the way that he treated you and only experienced loving good parents, you would have no need to think of killing people to protect your sister. This is simply how evil works; I believe that sometimes only bad can beat bad. I am not saying that you are all bad Jack so don't get me wrong. The fact is your badness comes from protecting good, and sometimes good isn't strong enough to beat evil alone. "

"So you think that I am bad, because I am meant to fight bad with bad?" "Well it is possible Jack. I believe everything happens for a reason. You said yourself that your dad's beatings made you stronger, strong enough to stop your father's evil actions towards your sister." "Well yes, I suppose you are right. Amy wasn't physically strong enough to take him on." "Exactly, so you had no choice to defend her Jack."

Jack thought about what the Bishop was saying and actually felt a bit better. "But what about the pedophile I killed; the nurse who was killing the old people in the hospital; and my latest killing, which I have to admit I enjoyed the most, my sister's attacker? Were those killings OK too Bishop? I mean I actually tortured those people! With my dad it was bad thoughts. I didn't actually kill him, but I want to. Tell me Bishop. Is that OK?"

"I am a Bishop. I am not God Jack. Is it OK that the children have been saved from the pedophile? Is it OK that the pensioners have been saved from the evil nurse? Is it OK that your sister's attacker can no longer attack women? Well if I was to answer those questions, my answer is yes. It is OK. You can only be wrong Jack, if you ask the wrong questions. Do you understand?" "No. I am not sure I do. I have just told you I kill people Bishop. You haven't told me I am wrong. I live in luxury. I enjoy what I do, and you haven't told me that I am wrong."

"You give to your community. You protect vulnerable people. And you don't molest kids, kill pensioners, or attack young women for fun. Now people that do those things just because they want to are wrong Jack. But who am I to judge. I am a Bishop. I work for God. That doesn't make me God. I cannot and will not condone or judge your actions. It is you that has to judge. It is you that has to judge you, no one else Jack. If you felt at the time you were doing good, then how can I say you wasn't. At the time of those killings you felt good, because you thought that you were getting rid of evil people. You were not wrong to think that, as you actually were." Jack couldn't believe what he was hearing. He was ready to throw in the towel;

he was ready to give up killing people, but now the Bishop was making him feel differently. Maybe this was the answer he was looking for.

He wasn't looking for someone to tell him he was right. Jack was looking for someone to tell him that he wasn't wrong. He felt so much better, like the weight of the world had been lifted from his shoulders. Jack came here for answers, and he got them. He stood up, took a wad of cash from his pocket, and handed it to the Bishop. "Thank you Bishop. I see clearly now." The bishop took the money and said, "No Jack. Thank you my son." With that Jack left the church feeling lighter, and the Bishop left the church feeling rather flush. Jack was now ready to go and see Amy. He wanted to tell her that her attacker was gone for good; he wanted to take her in his arms and tell her that she need not worry anymore. Jack was going to help fix her. To help Amy move on he decided that he needed to lay to rest some more personal shit. He needed to do what he should have done years ago. Jack needed to get to the route of all evil. He needed to pay a visit to mum and dad, but this wouldn't be the family reunion that they expected.

ABOUT THE AUTHOR

Layla Lowe is a parent of two beautiful children. She has always lived in Bedford, Bedfordshire. Layla is also a fulltime medical secretary, with a secret passion to be a writer. This is her debut book.

65863428R00070

Made in the USA
Charleston, SC
06 January 2017